The Enchanted City

The Enchanted City
A Journey to Lake Tanganyika

by
Eugène Hennebert

translated, annotated and introduced by
Brian Stableford

A Black Coat Press Book

Edited by Peter Gabbani

English adaptation and introduction Copyright © 2014 by Brian Stableford.
Cover illustration Copyright © 2014 Mike Hoffman.

Visit our website at www.blackcoatpress.com

Introduction

La Ville enchantée, voyage au Lac Tanganyika,
here translated as *The Enchanted City: A Journey to
Lake Tanganyika,* was published in Tours by Alfred
Mame et fils in 1885 under the pseudonym "M. Prévost-
Duclos," and was reprinted several times, including further Mame editions in 1888, 1890 and 1893 and a feuilleton version in *La Science Illustrée* in 1894. According
to the website of Le Club Verne, an affiliate of the Association des Amis du Roman Populaire, its author, Lieu-
tenant-Colonel Eugène Hennebert (1826-1896), had
originally penned a version of it under the title *Un drame
au centre de l'Afrique,* signed with the pseudonym Léopold Robert, and had sent a copy to Jules Verne in 1880;
he then rewrote it in accordance with Verne's sugges-
tions. The "Léopold Robert" version was not published,
and Hennebert does not appear to have published anything under that name.

Hennebert had previously supplied Alfred Mame
with another, more pedestrian, African adventure story
under the Prévost-Duclos name (which he improvised by
combining the surnames of two famous 18th century
novelists), *Une Aventure à Tombouctou* [An Adventure
in Timbuktu] (1882). A third short novel printed under a
version of the same pseudonym (omitting the hyphen,
thus making "Prévost" resemble a forename), "Les Pirates du désert" [The Pirates of the Desert], appeared as
a 22-part feuilleton in the *Journal des Voyages* (1886),
but was not reprinted in book form. The writing of these
various works of fiction must have seemed to Hennebert
to be a matter of relaxation from his more serious em-

ployments as a professional soldier and military theorist, but as *jeux d'esprit* go, they are by no means devoid of seriousness of purpose and attitude, and they are compiled methodically, with the kind of discipline one might expect from a strategist, as well as a breezy spirit of amusement.

Although *La Ville enchantée* might have been Hennebert's most widely read work, he was far more famous during his lifetime, and is now primarily remembered, as a military historian and commentator. His most important historical document consists of his accounts of the siege of Paris in 1870-71 and the Commune of 1871, written from the viewpoint of an officer in the Army of Versailles, which eventually overthrew the Communards; they were initially signed "Major H. de Sarrepont" but were reprinted under his own name when he was no longer on active service. His studies of the military potential of torpedoes, including *Les Torpilles* [Torpedoes] (1874 as Sarrepont; revised 1888 under his own name) and *Art militaire sous-aquatique* [The Art of Subaquatic Warfare] (1880 as Sarrepont) are also notable, as are his conscientious account of *L'Art militaire et science: le matériel de guerre moderne* [Military Art and Science: The Equipment of Modern Warfare] (1888) and his ominously-titled *La Guerre imminente: la défense du territoire* [The Imminent War: The Defense of Territory] (1890). Those of his non-fiction books most closely related to the subject matter of *La Ville enchantée* are, however, the ones dealing with ancient warfare rather than modern and future warfare, most notably *Histoire Militaire des animaux* [A Military History of Animals] (1893).

The decision by the editor of *La Science Illustrée*, Louis Figuier, to reprint a novel in his *roman scientifique* feuilleton slot that was currently in print, and had been continuously in print for nearly a decade, is a curious one, but might reflect the difficulty he was having in finding Vernian fictions with a hint of the *scientifique* about them, even though the most obvious rival market for that kind of work, the *Journal des Voyages*, preferred straightforward adventure stories. In spite of its outré setting, *La Ville enchantée* is no more unlikely than many of the serials published in the *Journal des Voyages*, and it does have the advantages of seeming solidly researched and of paying homage to many of the heroes of the heroic age of African exploration, which must have appealed to Figuier, who was always interested in the didactic aspects of the fiction he published. *La Ville enchantée* also gives the impression of having benefited from Verne's input, maintaining a buoyant tone and a hectic narrative pace throughout its action-packed plot, cruising at a melodramatic pitch that many supposedly Vernian novels failed to reach, let alone sustain for long.

Like numerous other items that Figuier published under the *roman scientifique* rubric, *La Ville enchantée* is not speculative fiction, and does not, therefore, qualify as "proto-science fiction," but it is thoroughly impregnated with scientific materials, not merely in terms of the various informational materials on which its widely-read scientist Professor Cornelius draws, but in the propensity of all the characters to problem-solving. In their long conflict with the vast army that lays siege to Kisimbasimba, the eponymous "enchanted city," all the characters, including the enterprising cook who tends to scramble the random items of factual information he has at his disposal in an absurd manner, think in scientific terms, both theoretically and practically, because that is the very essence of their civilization, as opposed to their enemies' barbarity.

It is true that Hennebert's fictitious ambassadors of science and civilization receive help that seems uncanny, if not frankly supernatural, from the various animal and human inhabitants of the "enchanted" city, without which their scientific expertise would be impotent to counter the vast numerical advantage of the barbarian horde, but their ingenuity and technology play a major role nevertheless. As the plot unfolds, it always seems likely that the mercurial city-dwellers might have every reason to thank their civilized collaborators for their assistance in staving off disaster, if disaster is ultimately to be avoided even partly, in what is bound to be a desperately difficult contest.

There is much in the novel that now seems rather naïve, although it must have seemed rather advanced and daring in its own day, and much that now seems uncomfortably racist, although it is considerably less so than the vast majority of contemporary works of popular fiction. The heroic age of African exploration inevitably appears to be very distant indeed in the post-colonial era, but that seeming naivety is compensated by the fact that it lends novels celebrating the achievements of the era a definite nostalgia value. *La Ville enchantée*, when it was eventually published, was exactly contemporary with H. Rider Haggard's *King Solomon's Mines*, billed in London at the time as "the most amazing book ever written." The latter founded an entire subgenre of African adventures, in which it was only ever outshone by the same author's monumental *She* (1887), and it makes Hennebert's novel look a trifle staid in spite of its narrative pace and flamboyance.

La Ville enchantée nevertheless makes an interesting comparison with Haggard's classic, not only because of certain points of coincidental similarity, but also because of a marked contrast in attitude, which forbids the conscientious Hennebert to make use of some of the melodramatic narrative moves of which Haggard made so much, even though many of them are set up and foreshadowed within his plot. Whereas the treasure of the legendary mines remains a key object of the plot's focus throughout Haggard's novel, even though the rewards actually distributed to various members of the cast are quite different, material concerns are never an issue in Hennerbert's novel; when the characters stumble across gold nuggets, they simply disregard them as a complete irrelevance. Even the intriguing mysteries of Kisimbasimba's ancient past are set aside; Professor Cornelius is strangely uninterested in the more Romantic implications of the city's existence—an indifference that cannot be entirely excused by the hectic pace of the life-threatening events in which he is caught up—and there is a stubborn practicality about Hennebert's manner of dealing with exotic subject matter that is quite unlike Haggard's ever-readiness to marvel.

It is hardly surprising, given the plotting opportunities that Hennebert so conscientiously set aide, that Haggard, who never missed such tricks, went on to cultivate a worldwide fame in the adventure story genre, matched only by Jules Verne's, while "M. Prévost-Duclos" vanished into obscurity after his one moderate success. *La Ville enchantée* is an intriguing novel nevertheless, by no means unworthy of a significant place in the canon of African adventure fiction, by virtue of its narrative quality as well as its status as a pioneer. In spite of its occasional pretentiousness and didactic fervor, it is essentially an item of what would nowadays be thought of as "pulp fiction," but in terms of the artistry of that unjustly-slandered medium, it made a worthy contribution to the evolution of its subgenre, and it remains very readable today, in spite of the sophistication of narrative technique that has taken place in the long interim.

This translation has been made from the copy of the 1893 reprint of the Mame edition reproduced on the Bibliothèque Nationale's *gallica* website. The translation was difficult, not only because of the number of African terms, many of which are rendered by the author in an orthography that is no longer current, but also because one of the major characters spices his speech with mangled Latin and another with awkward Arabic, while the ubiquitous Isidore frequently indulges in untranslatable wordplay, and accidentally gives rise to other jokes with his mistaken juxtapositions of historical characters and events. I have retained the author's spelling of most African names, retaining his use of *ou* in many instances where modern spelling prefers *u*, but have substituted modern equivalents when the latter are likely to be familiar to the reader—using Zulu rather than Zoulou, for instance. I have done my best to preserve the flavor of the original and not to burden the text with too many explanatory footnotes, although some readers might feel that I have not had much success in the latter task.

Brian Stableford

THE ENCHANTED CITY

Chapter I
The Demons of the Lake

On 13 March 1877, in the heart of equatorial Africa, the first rays of dawn illuminated the prelude to one of those dramas that the journals of great voyagers only insert in terms full of fear.

The scene was about to unfold not far from Cape Nyonngo, whose white point, like the prow of a ship, cuts neatly into the waters of Lake Tanganyika at 27°30 east longitude and 3°23 south latitude.

A confused mass of tortuous and profoundly-ravined ridges, the bulk of the cape is dominated by a vast plateau, the arid soil of which nourishes only a single tree, but a giant of the kind. It is a baobab whose leafy crown measures no less than a hundred and fifty meters in circumference, and which, under that immense mass of branches, could easily shelter an entire regiment from the rain. The trunk of that sovereign among vegetables is bizarrely carved around its perimeter. Guided by the spirit of whimsy that presides over the execution of infantile works, temeritous hands have sculpted a number of monsters with human faces there, in the thickness of the bark, with an artistry that bears no resemblance to that if our master woodcarvers. Those images, unpleasant to behold, are framed by hideous realities: chaplets of freshly severed heads, festoons of tresses scalped from enemies and garlands of skulls that time has polished like ivory.

Thus, on the thirteenth of March, at daybreak, three prisoners had just been attached to the foot of the baobab on the plateau of Nyonngo, solidly tied with the aid of ropes of aloe fiber mixed with tiger grass. One of those unfortunates was white, another of Semitic blood with a negro tint, and the third a mulatto.

The white man seemed to be about twenty-eight years of age. Of medium height and robust constitution, he had a high forehead, brown eyes and a Grecian nose following the principles of esthetics. His lips were a trifle thin, but did not advertise any malevolence. His mouth even sketched an excellent smile—a sad smile, but still proud, which allowed a glimpse of two rows of dazzling pearly white teeth. A crow's wing beard, smooth and bushy, set off his sun-tanned complexion advantageously. Coiffed in a hat made of reed stems, clad in a tunic and trousers in grey wool, he wore a buffalo hide belt around his waist.

The black man, who seemed to be about thirty, was tall and respectably plump; his hands were delicate and chubby. He had a broad forehead, fleshy cheeks, a double chin and beautiful long-lashed eyes with a tender and profound gaze. His face radiated calm and placidity. His costume did not differ much from that of Algerian Arabs; he wore a red skullcap on his head with a silken *h'aik* and a black camel-hide *brima*. Two or three burnooses were superimposed on his body; on his legs, red morocco boots each affected the form of the trunk of a banana tree. A chaplet of large beads hung around his neck, descending to the middle of his chest.

The mulatto was a tall lanky fellow, thin and stiff, with a slightly arched back. The uncommon length of his legs gave his gait some analogy with that of the wading bird known as a secretary bird. His head, rather broad at the height of his cheekbones, took on the shape of a quadrangular pyramid in the cranial region, gently rounded at the summit. His ears were gigantic; his eyes presented the particular obliquity typical of the natives of the Congo; his lower jaw was equipped with long and pointed teeth. His physiognomy was suggestive of a humble and timid character. As for his mode of dress, it was absolutely grotesque.

In fact, the bare-headed and barefooted mulatto wore tight trousers with yellow piping and a huge red jacket, probably plundered from one of Queen Victoria's horse-guards. The jacket was tightened at the wait by means of a belt—or, rather, a rope—from which was suspended, by a little leather thong, a pocketknife of a study kind. Another rope or strap was passed over the shoulder of the red coat, whose two ends were fixed to a canvas bag like the *musettes* in which the cavalrymen of French regiments keep their grooming equipment. In sum, the tall fellow was decked out in a fashion resembling, save for his height, one of the monkeys paraded around by organ grinders.

Around the three prisoners bound to the baobab, a multitude of delirious individuals were stamping their feet, uttering blood-curdling howls. They were black-skinned men of medium height, but of a type very different from the vulgar native with the flat nose, thick lips and curly hair. On the contrary, they had flat hair, long eyelashes, bushy eyebrows, keen eyes profoundly sunk in their orbits, a straight nose, thin lips and small ears.

An enormous torso, broad hips and thin legs collaborated in giving them an extremely original appearance.

Dressed, for the most part, in the skins of big cats, the rest of the body was smeared with white, red and blue, the three colors of war in the regions of central Africa. A few guinea fowl or green pigeon feathers were stuck in the hair. Some of them wore little mantles of bark on their shoulders, with a kind of wolf-skin cape. On their knees and ankles there were bracelets with wooden bells; on their wrists, ivory rings; on their heads, turbans or crowns of wisteria. Finally, a few, aristocratic in their bearing, were clad in white fleecy goatskin skirts and mantles made of hedgehog skin, with their lower legs fringed with brass bells. Their coiffure consisted of fur caps ornamented with glass beads and a red feather. From the center of that headdress emerged a long hank of hair, thrown backwards following the arc of a circle, from which a large bouquet of goat hair was suspended.

In the first rank of the bloodthirsty blacks, a chain of horrible women was agitating, summarily dressed in small goatskin aprons edged with little bells made with iron hoops. By way of ornament, those harpies had fixed bunched of sun-dried lizards to their heads.

Bursts of savage music cruelly accompanied the overture of the drama anticipated by the spectators. Applied to the mouths of artistes with robust lungs, long buffalo horns cast sonorous waves to the winds that collided violently. The rhythm of the funeral march was beaten by vigorous hands on leopard-skin war drums, sheet metal bells and leather bucklers. All the instruments of the orchestra combined their effects in accordance with astonishing principles, to which our professors of harmony have doubtless never had the idea of exposing their pupils.

Suddenly, in response to an imperceptible signal, the din calmed down.

An old man, a woman and a young man detached themselves from the furious circle.

Clad in a long white robe, the old man had a kind of dolman on his shoulders made of human hair; a small copper bell tinkled at the end of each of those carefully combed banks, heightened with glass beads. His head disappeared beneath an enormous tuft of ostrich feathers; his torso was ornamented with chaplets of teeth. In his hand he was holding a large white weapon with several blades, similar to a short-handled halberd. That long-bearded old man was the *kilombe*, the chief of the national magicians.

The woman's only garment was a kind of girdle from which were suspended leather thongs ornamented with shells, teeth and coral. The rest of her body was tattooed with diamond shapes. Every hair on her head was threaded through a number of cylindrical glass beads, somewhat reminiscent of fragments of pipe stem. In her left hand she held a small buckler shaped like a violin; in the right was a lance with a flaxen tuft for a pennon. The hideous virago was an eminent sorceress.

The young man sported a large pink shell on his forehead and a sheep's horn at each of his temples; on his breast he wore a bison horn tied with a piece of cord to a zebra hoof. He was carrying a *troumbache*, a weapon made of black wood, flat in form and pointed at either end. The young man—or, rather, the adolescent—was a simple *ganga*, a run-of-the-mill magician who, by reason of his special armament, was known as a *troumbachaganga*.

There was a profound silence.

The three individuals marched at a solemn pace toward the baobab, making ostentatious genuflections before the images sculpted in the bark of the tree. Those graffiti represented Loubari, the African Satan; Mgoussa, the evil spirit; and Mousammouira, the spirit of storms.

Having piously invoked the demons of Tanganyika, the three magicians prepared to torture the prisoners in accordance with local custom. The troumbachaganga took up the position of someone about to throw in a game of darts. The tattooed harpy pointed her lance like a fencing foil. The kilombe, twirling his blade, took up a stance with his legs braced, ready to leap forward.

Chapter II
The Gamble of Those Condemned to Death

How had the unfortunates who were about to play the part of bloody sacrifices to the Spirits of the Lake come to be lost in the heart of the African continent? The three poor wretches, attached to the service of a great voyager, had, one might say, fallen on the battlefield of fidelity and devotion. For two years they had followed their master, sharing in his good and bad fortune, and now found themselves separated from him for the first time. One day, they had allowed themselves to be taken by surprise and overrun by a dense band of blacks; overwhelmed by the weight of their numbers, they had been captured.

The white foreigner answered to the name of Isidore Chauvelot—a name that betrayed his nationality. He was, in fact, a Frenchman, and a Frenchman of the Var, a native of Six-Fours, the beautiful eagle's nest that overlooks the bay of Toulon, coquettishly reflected in the blue waters of Saint Nazaire.

Isidore was the cook of the dispersed expedition. The senior personnel prized his talents highly, and that was only just. After an initial apprenticeship served at the Hôtel de la Croix-de-Malte in Toulon, and then at the Hôtel des Colonies in Marseilles, he had taken lessons from an eminent professor in Toulouse, who had revealed to him the secrets of the art, particularly the formula for a certain Sinhalese curry that had made him famous. Finally, he had gone to Paris to complete his studies. By dint of hard work, perseverance and genius, he had ended up working at the Grand Hôtel in the capacity of *sous-chef*. It was there that the Sultan of Zanzibar, wonderstruck by his guinea fowl with Haitian sauce, had attempted to woo him away with the offer of a host of considerable dignities, notably that of director-general of his fishponds, gardens, pheasantries, poultry yards and aviaries.

The *sous-chef*, whose success was celebrated by the Parisian press, had declined all those honors—but then, bored and weary of the asphalt horizons of Paris that he had perpetually before his eyes, tormented by the spirit of adventure, he had allowed himself to be collected by voyagers—Frenchmen, those!—who were bravely going to explore the heart of Africa.

To complete that biography, it is necessary to say that, interrupting the course of his studies one day, the cook had done a stint in the 1st zouaves in the capacity of drummer. History also records that the doctor of sauces was a crack shot with a rifle. The echoes of the Kasbah of Medeah have conserved the memory of the brio that distinguished his manner of beating the reveille and rolling out mortal fire.

As if those instrumental and culinary talents were not sufficient, nature had also endowed young Isidore with a host of solid qualities. He was, it may be said, an excellent fellow, regular in his conduct, absolutely sober, limiting his pleasure to cigarettes, of which, to tell the truth, he was a heavy smoker. He always seemed cheerful, even something of a joker, always philosophical and full of enthusiasm. Unfortunately, these perfections were eclipsed, more than once a day, by the mists of one intolerable fault: Isidore was prodigiously vain. His vanity, moreover, revealed itself in a singular fashion. He, who had only ever had to go pale beneath the works of the

Cuisinière bourgeoise and other technical treatises of the same stripe had—who would have believed it?—immense pretentions in matters of literature and ineradicable pretentions to intuitive science, especially in matters of history, politics and geography.

His discourse, moreover, testified to an admirably incoherent education. His schoolmaster had taught him a little about everything and very little about anything in particular, all without any method or determined plan, making him read publications of all sorts: stories of voyages, cheap newspapers, novels and poetry, carefully refraining from seasoning his pupil's reading with any kind of critical observation. Isidore had drunk cheerfully from all these springs; he had furnished his brain with a host of variegated fragments, had made the mountain of Six-Fours into a Parnassus populated with muses who twittered like linnets and reasoned like crows.

As for any slightly rational enchainment of ideas, he scarcely paid any heed to it, intrepidly coupling, at the risk of making them howl, words that made a natural contrast, committing to memory prodigious anachronisms, making stews of the most disparate morsels. Knowing a little about a great many disparate things, he firmly believed that he knew everything; he was intent on passing for a superior man and never ceased to complain about the ill luck that prevented him from emerging from obscurity.

The pretentious ignoramus annoyed his masters by professing incredible enormities in a loud voice, and his comrades by heaping them with disdain. How many times had he not treated as simpletons the poor companions now attached, as he was, to a baobab?

The black man to the right of the arrogant cook was named Mimoun-ben-Abdallah. He was an Algerian Arab. Born in El Kseur in the south, he had served in the Senegal spahis. With regard to the commander of the expedition Mimoun served the functions of hunter; with remarkable skill, he regularly brought venison to the camp. He was a zealous Muslim, always calm, absorbed in contemplation, resigned to the will of Allah, only opening his mouth to emit verses from the Koran.

The mulatto placed to Isidore's left had been baptized Choka, a name that the facetious cook had rapidly transformed into Chocolat. The son of a native woman from Saint Paul de Loanda,[1] Chocolat had been brought up by a Portuguese missionary, but the fruits of that distinguished education were reduced to a few fragments of Latin with which he enameled his speech and his practices of puerile devotion at San José de Cacuaco.[2] Forgetting the reverend's serious lessons, in the school of the bush, the eccentric had not taken long to mold himself on the model of the Bohemian that one encounters in all the ports on the African coast, and whom the English call by the generic denomination of Jack-Jack.

Ordinarily, having no other domicile than the harbor steps, jack-jacks exercise, in turn or simultaneously, a host of different professions, according to the weather, fortune or opportunity. They are, as the whim takes them, street porters, domestic servants, messengers, cri-

---

[1] I have retained the author's Frenchified version of the name of the chief seaport and capital city of Angola, then known as São Paulo da Assunção de Loanda and nowadays simply known as Luanda.

[2] Again, I have retained the author's version of what appears to be a conflation of the names of two local villages long since swallowed up by the city of Luanda, São José do Calumbo and Cacuaco.

ers, sailors, and chiefs of pagazis or baggage porters. It was thus that Chocolat had been picked up on the dock at Saint Paul and enrolled in the capacity of laborer. As often as not, Isidore took possession of him to pluck fowl, peel vegetables, wash the saucepans or turn the handle of the coffee grinder.

The excellent jack-jack lent himself readily to everything that was asked of him, for he was naturally obliging, mild and timid; but he also had good reasons for being obliging in the functions of scullion, the accomplishment of which was always worth a few meager rewards of scraps and leftovers. The poor fellow was afflicted by the malady known as hunger sickness; he ate incessantly, but incessantly thought that he was on the point of starvation.

In the course of the preparations for their torture, the three designated victims adopted different attitudes.

Chocolat, dying of hunger, was on the point of falling unconscious, sighing as he cast his gaze toward the zenith, where he perceived, oscillating over his head, the beautiful fruits of the baobab, which measure no less than thirty centimeters in length, and are known as "monkey-bread."[3] He was weeping, and scarcely had the strength to invoke San José de Cacuaco in bad Latin.

Mimoun, more than ever confided to resignation, never ceased to murmur: "Allahu Akbar!"—God is great.

As for Isidore, he muttered to himself, not without arrogance: "Oh, these savages...! These savages who

---

[3] The fruits of the baobab, *Adansonia digitata*, were indeed known as *pain de singe* [monkey-bread] at the time, but are not to be confused with the modern American pastry to which the same name was applied in the 1950s.

want my skin are beasts…my God, are they beasts! There's not one of them who seems to understand! Oh, it's more than a crime they're going to commit here; it's a sin, as Buffon said—for, after all, I'm not just anyone. To think that they're going to put an end to a man like me!"

Then these gusts of pride *in extremis* were chased away by fits of sinister laughter. "They're going to devour us, of course," Isidore added, "but to want to eat me, a cook…that's too much! And you, Chocolat, you great simpleton, who can't do anything but cry famine, wait a little…they're going to invite you to dinner! Don't worry, we're going to be served…to these Messieurs of the Black Band…!"

It was at the moment that these strangled words emerged from Isidore's mouth that the sacrificers were about to strike their victims. The harpy, brandishing her lance, was making abominable grimaces at Mimoun's beard, when the strident sound of a horn rang out.

Then the scene changed

The entire audience, sorceress and gangas included, fell face down on the ground, as if moved by a spring. There was no longer anything around the baobab but humbly prostrated people, their arms extended at right angles to their bodies, uttering howls like distressed dogs.

Chapter III
A Savage's Good Idea

Whence came that sudden calm in the ocean of black heads, formerly so stormy? Why was that blood-thirsty crowd no longer thinking of anything but biting the dust? It was because they had heard, not without terror, the blast of the ivory horn, and because the piercing sound of that Oliphant announced to all and sundry the approach of a redoubtable chief, a great Mata Sonapanga.

A new character did indeed make his entrance onto the stage: a tall young man with a handsome face, but a ferocious expression, then lips and an icy gaze. Following the fashion of Kittara,[4] he had had the incisors of his lower jaw removed. His wiry hair was cut very short; he had, however, retained on his head, from the occiput to the sinciput, a dense forest five or six centimeters long. From that fashion of coiffure a caterpillar resulted similar to the crest of a Bavarian helmet—a caterpillar prolonged over the shoulders by the tail of a zebra, forming a mane. That tail was constellated by vulgar glass beads.

The Sonapanga wore enormous earrings made of beads of opaline porcelain the size of a green pigeon's egg; a robe of bark beneath an overcoat made of antelope skins; a necklace and bracelets of small glass beads;

---

[4] The kingdom of Kittara, which occupied a tract of land that is now mostly in Uganda, although it extends westwards into the Democratic Republic of the Congo and southwards into Tanzania, had long decayed and disintegrated by 1877, but was still remembered with a certain reverence.

gaiters of kimaraphamba beads; and a brass wire ring on each of his fingers and each of his toes. In his hand he held a cane of pandana palm, which served him as a scepter; his Oliphant, hanging over his shoulder, was bouncing on his left hip.

The terrible great chief solemnly picked his way through the flattened crowd. He advanced followed by an immense cortege. Immediately behind him marched women laden with his armor and his offensive weapons. The famous song about Marlborough[5] seemed to have been made expressly for those living panoplies, for one of them carried a troumbache, another a koubbeda; yet others were laden with javelins and bucklers. There were also some who were not carrying anything, and the latter were no less beautiful. One might have thought them bronze castings of the Venus de Medici.

After them came the bodyguards, then the representatives of the sacerdotal caste, the official magicians, preceded by the great fetisher and the chief omen-reader. They were followed by the council of the elders and a multitude of courtiers.

What was he seeking on the plateau of Nyonngo, that savage chief surrounded by his general staff? Had he come, avid with emotion, to witness the torture of the prisoners? No, for human blood entered into his regime, so to speak; everyday he had a few of his men tortured or put to death. Had he arrived beneath the baobab with the intention of offering even greater sacrifices to Moussammouira, Loubari or Mgoussa? That was scarcely probable; he was in no hurry to bend his knee before the frightful images that represented the demons of the lake.

---

[5] The French folk song *Malbrough s'en va-t-en guerre*.

His intentions did not take long to become manifest. Instead of proceeding with preliminary ceremonies he headed straight for the tree, scanned the poor fellow condemned to death with a circular glance, and, addressing himself specifically to the white man, he questioned him sharply in good Kiswahili, the original idiom that Max Müller classifies in the eastern group of Bantu languages. It is, at any rate, spoken on the coast of Zanzibar, from which it has spread to the interior of Africa. It is also understood beyond the great equatorial lakes. Fortunately, Isidore knew a few fragments of it, which he seasoned agreeably with locutions borrowed from Algerian Sabir.[6] That simple linguistic baggage permitted the former zouave not only to understand the Mata Sonapanga but even, with the aid of gestures to make himself sufficiently understood.

"Mericani?" said the chief, in a caressing voice.

"No, no, not Mericani!" protested the condemned man, swiftly. "Make no mistake, Monsieur Mata…me Francis!"

To understand the commencement of the interrogation that the noble individual was undertaking, it is necessary to know that for the blacks of Central Africa, all white foreigners are Americans. The English of Saint Paul de Loanda, Zanzibar, Albert and Victoria-Nyanza are unceremoniously included in that generic denomination. Concurrently, the Africans attribute to white men the designation *mousoungou*."

"Mousoungou?" the young native continued, in the most honeyed tone.

_____

[6] Sabir [literally "science" or "knowledge"] was a pidgin employed all around the Mediterranean coast as a *lingua franca* from the 11th to the 19th century.

"Right, Mousoungou—I prefer that! Yes, I won't try to hide it; I'm a man with a pale face. So what?"

"Death! Death!"

"I'm going to be killed? I suspected as much. Do you think I'm blind?"

"But you prophet of the god Ouaka."

"Impossible! Me, a prophet...! Go on. What do you mean?"

"Life! Life!"

"We're not going to be killed? Well, of course, that's a good idea! In fact, now that I think about it, one doesn't kill prophets. If one killed them, they wouldn't prophesy, and as one wants them to prophesy...."

The Mata Sonapanga was offering to let Isidore live, but he did not hide the fact that he expected good and important services from him.

He explained to the prisoner, obligingly, that he commanded considerable forces, an entire people marching from the east to the west across the African continent; that the army in question was divided into seven corps of seventy thousand men each; that his power was absolutely irresistible; that Ouaka, the ruler of the sky, had promised to submit all the land in Africa to the domination of the Ormas—that was the name of his people.

Nevertheless, a disagreeable little cloud that was darkening the horizon opened so splendidly to the conqueror. Three days from the plateau of Nyonngo, where his general quarters were, there was a great fortress or *banza* on the Tanganyika that had stopped his march dead and prevented him from pushing his conquests any further. That inconvenient banza he had tried hard to take; he had blockaded it narrowly by land and on the water, but in vain. The accursed place opposed an invisible resistance to his efforts. His water-borne flotillas had tightened their moorings in vain; his besieging troops had grown weary without any profit in the lines of Kifoukourou.

According to the Sonapanga, the impregnable fortress was named Kisimbasimba, the city of lions. No sound escaped from the place; never had the shadow of a human being been glimpsed at any point on its ramparts. It was surely devoid of inhabitants, absolutely deserted. And yet, by night, its walls lit up, and were populated by monsters and by phantoms. Globes of fire emerged therefrom, which snaked through the surrounding area for a long way. Its large and profound ditches were nothing but the lairs of wild beasts; hailstorms of stones fell from its extraordinary battlements, rains of venomous creatures and deluges of improbable grapeshot!

It was easy to imagine how, in consequence, the troops at the camp of Kifoukourou had been tested, demoralized and discouraged. The men were beginning to claim that the mysterious banza was nothing other than a city haunted by demons, by the Spirits of the Lake. And it was to appease the furious anger of those evil spirits that the army stationed on the plateau of Nyonngo had thought it as well to offer as a holocaust Isidore, Mimoun and Chocolat.

Having posed the problem, the Sonapanga formulated his conclusions. The chief magician of his general quarters had just revealed to him that the most malign spirits were absolutely impotent against men with pale faces; that the Mericanis, and, in general, all mousoungou, were more malign than the spirits, powerful as they were supposed to be; that they were capable of any undertaking, and any success; that they knew everything, even how to take the banza that was resisting in an indecent manner; that the white prisoner they had in their hands had been providentially sent by Ouaka.

In sum, the young chief offered the cook life, liberty and fortune if he would take possession of Kisimbasimba.

"Well," said Isidore, "word of honor, that's something I wasn't expecting!"

The former drummer in the zouaves, having never doubted himself in the slightest, did not even take the trouble to reflect. He did not have a second of hesitation, and felt without restraint that he was an expert in the art of attacking strongholds.

"It's no trouble," he declared, with magnificent assurance. "No trouble at all. The banzas of Africa I know. This one's no better than the rest, and I'll soon settle its hash, even if it is a city of lions. As for the rest, let's not talk about it—it's a load of nonsense and your men are seeing things. I promise you than in two days, you'll be able to smoke your calumet on the boulevards of this enchanted city, for I'll have cleared out all its spirits and its wild beasts once and for all!"

At these words, the Sonapanga, arming himself with a small knife, cut the prisoners' bonds personally. At a signal from his *barghoumi*, the crowd, still prostrate on the ground, got up briskly. On the orders they received to make a racket, the musicians started to bang their most sonorous metallic instruments with mighty blows of the fist.

The cook, who had been within two inches of death a few moments before, was solemnly proclaimed *ganga-ya-ita*—which is to say, Minister of War and Generalissimo.

"Yes indeed!" he said to himself, with imperturbable seriousness. "That's a promotion, and no mistake! To pass from the rank of laboratory chef to general in chief is what one might call taking a step forward in life."

Mimoun, to whom the sorceress was still showing her teeth, simply put his hand on his heart and murmured in a placid tone: "Alhamdulillah!"—God be praised.

As for Chocolat, he did not take the time to recognize, in that occurrence, the intervention of his usual protector, San José de Cacuaco. Feeling the freedom of his long fingers, he hastened to plunge them into his supply bag. From the depths of the sack he extracted, voluptuously, a Lyon sausage, of which he only made three mouthfuls.

Chapter IV
His Excellency Isidore

The camp on the plateau of Nyonngo was formed of hamlets arranged in a defensive formation and a few fenced areas, large circular enclosures known in Africa as *bomas*. Inside each enclosure, symmetrically arranged in concentric circles, was a multitude of huts built from mimosa branches and woven tiger grass. Their cylindrical form and conical roofs with which they were coiffed made them resemble beehives, and that form was in harmony with their purpose, for they sheltered invaders, black hornets with human faces.

Each boma was pierced with a dozen gates, next to each of which stood a special hut known as an *ihouanza*, endowed with the dual function of guard post and café. It was there that warriors of distinction came to drink *pommbé*, a detestable indigenous beer that they savored with delight while pursuing the course of their interminable palavers.

A special boma housed the Sonapanga's general quarters. In the center of the fenced enclosure stood a large rectangular building with four walls, supported by outhouses. That was the great chief's palace. Another boma served as a park for his elephants.

Isidore was hastily provided with an elegant hut, from the top of which flew a banner of red cloth. Inside, the ground was covered by a lion skin carpet. A neighboring hut was allocated to Mimoun and Chocolat; another served as a baggage store. The booty taken from the prisoners was restored to them almost integrally;

they found all their bales, with the exception of some cases of rum, which the Sonapanga thought he ought to keep, in order to drink to the fortunate deliverance of the foreigners.

When that installation was complete, it was solemnly followed by the investiture of His Excellency Isidore, in conformity with the national etiquette. A long red mantle charged with glass beads was thrown over the shoulders of the ganga-ya-ita; he was coiffed in a felt hat with a crest of ostrich and parrot feathers; he was armed with a spear with a shaft of reed acacia and a large cavalry saber of European provenance; finally, a sack was hung on his back. He thought so for a moment, but it was not a beautiful handmaiden with which he was being gratified, but a bronze footstool like those that the petty kings of central Africa always carry in order to be able to sit down during battles.

Given the absolute lack of horses, the new Excellency received by way of a mount one of the Mata Sonapanga's elephants, a magnificent beast, admirably well trained, answering to the name of Moonchild. She wore a sheet of red cloth heightened with glass beads and large porcelain beads; her forehead and ears had been painted with the colors of war; a host of multicolored plumes floated around her enormous skull. On her back there was a *haoussah*, a kind of packsaddle edged with a low parapet like a handrail. That bulwark was garnished with white cotton decorated with red ribbons. On her neck sat a driver armed with an iron bar analogous in form to a whaler's harpoon. A Hindu by birth, the driver had been hired in Zanzibar.

Thus heaped with honors, wilting under the weight of his new dignities, the former drummer in the zouaves did not feel at ease. Taking his role seriously, he thought about reorganizing the army placed under his command, and, for a start, of constituting a service staff. Unfortunately, the personnel at his disposal were somewhat limited; all he were his two companions, Mimoun and Chocolat.

Isidore was not put off by such a small inconvenience.

"You've been a soldier," he said to Mimoun. "You're an old Senegal spahi, so you're familiar with military service. You'll be the chief of my general staff. It's up to the two of us to draw up plans, and to get out of trouble. A fine business!"

"Insha'Allah!"—If Allah permits—replied Mimoun sententiously.

"As for you, Chocolat, you great *vol-au-vent*, you've only ever served at table. What are you good for? Not much, undoubtedly…but since I can't do otherwise, I'll give you preferential treatment. You'll be my aide-de-camp, my orderly officer, my secretary and all the trimmings."

"Señor Isidore," the jack-jack observed, *"ego meschinello…nescio* the trimmings."[7]

"That's fine! No observations! Besides which, your new métier won't be difficult. I just have to buy you some shoulder knots. Don't worry, you'll get your braid, and with that, you'll see, everything will go like clockwork."

Having made these arrangements, the cook, generously abusing his ministerial authority, promised Mimoun the rank of colonel and Chocolat the rank of captain. The improvised colonel insisted on retaining his

---

[7] *Meschinello* is Italian rather than Latin, meaning an individual of little worth.

Arab costume, so elegant and so comfortable as it was beneath the African sky. He also hastened to add to it an excellent hunting rifle that he had found in his luggage, which he slung over his shoulder. Under the terms of a bizarre etiquette, the observation of which would have struck Speke with profound amazement, he was given by way of a battle charger a lovely milk cow with a black and white coat. The Africans have, as is evident, solved the equation cow = horse, so celebrated in the annals of schoolboy humor.

For the excellent Muslim, who was never astonished by anything, the sight of his baroque mount only brought to mind one of the hundred and fourteen surahs of the Koran, the one entitled "The Cow,"[8] in which there is mention of men who, "occupied uniquely in the concern of fighting in the path of God, have no means of enriching themselves by commerce."

As for Chocolat, who always did whatever was wanted, provided that he had provisions of food in his supply bag and a knife suspended from his belt, he consented to put on a new uniform, and received in consequence effects of clothing appropriate to his rank: a red woolen skirt, a mantle made of porcupine skin, a cap with jay plumes and a small short-handled hatchet. For a mount he had a small and plump gray saddle donkey, much less tall than his long legs.

With that, His Excellency decided that, as any good commanding general ought to do, he would hold a grand review of his troops the very next day. An important occasion!

---

[8] The reference is to the second surah [chapter] of the Koran, "Al-Baqara"

It was late. Having given orders and smoked a few cigarettes, Isidore lay down on the lion skins in order to go to sleep—but it was impossible for him to close his eyes because of the racket that was being made in the camp. The war drums, which had not stopped beating for a moment all day, continued to beat all night long. The sticks of the *gongongs* and the hammers that struck the iron hoop bells were plied by hands of steel. The drumbeats rumbled like thunderclaps.

The orchestra was comprised of no less than twenty-five brigades of fifteen musicians, and all those instrumentalists were elite virtuosos. What they were executing so intrepidly was a continuous serenade in honor of the new ganga-ya-ita. That being the case, the ganga-ya-ita Isidore could hardly permit himself to impose silence on those disturbers of the public peace; he could only chew his bit. That was what he did, while letting loose the flood of his maledictions against the frightful percussionists who had certainly not been to military school, since they were not playing any tune, could not distinguish their *fla* from their *ra*, and did not even know how to execute a *roll*.

In spite of the fatigues of a long night of insomnia, the former drummer of the 1st zouaves was up at daybreak, in full dress uniform.

Following the program he had traced out the day before, he had to commence his inspection with the troops of the lake flotilla. In consequence, he went down toward the Tanganyika with his chief of staff, Mimoun, his aide-de-camp, Chocolat, and a few Orma officers who served as his guides. The path he had to follow broke up into monotonous threads traced through fields of sorghum, alternating with fallow land, zones of red clay afflicted with sterility, and jungles of bamboo saplings and stunted rattan. To advance along that route invaded by tropical vegetation, it was necessary to defend oneself continually against rushes, ferns, trenchant stems that cut the traveler's face and lianas that wound around him or lacerated him.

Finally, they arrived at a little cove, where the pirogue was moored that had been sent by the admiral commanding the siege in the lake sector. They embarked immediately to go to the mooring lines that extended in front of the harbor of Kisimbasimba.

The lake is a very striking sight. Surrounded by high mountains in which red clay, sandstone and granite are dominant, the equatorial Caspian was framed at the level of the camp by a zone of verdure bordered by a ribbon of golden sand fringed with tall reeds. Its waters are of two shades, one sea-green and the other pale blue, which dissolves in places into a milky tint. When the wind rises, the Tanganyika is troubled; its waves, suddenly becoming green-tinted, break into a menacing surf.

It was a beautiful day. The waters of the lake had taken on their most azure hue. In the clear waters, whose depths Africans are unable to measure, hippopotamuses were playing, along with freshwater porpoises and a kind of seal or Nereid peculiar to equatorial lakes. For a while, the pirogue was obliged to draw away from the bank along which it was traveling because of the presence of a *tinghitinghi*, a vast mass of interlaced plants forming a bank uncrossable by any boat—a bank in the tangles of which legions of bullfrogs were swarming and bellowing.

Emerging from those sargassos, the pirogue continued its route and reached the mooring lines without any encumbrance. The Orma flotilla was comprised of war canoes and *daous*, larger craft—all of them prizes taken from river dwellers. Hollowed out from a single alikonda trunk, each of the canoes was manned by a hundred and thirty warriors. The daous, formed in a squadron as if for a sea cruise, were moved by the arms of forty oarsmen; each carried a hundred and fifty men, archers or riflemen. The hulls of the primitive ships had been painted in war colors—or, more precisely, daubed with red, white and blue clay. Their long swan's neck prows bore antelope horns at their summit, and between those forms were clumps of red and white parrot feathers.

The admiral's daou was called the *Magalarazi*; it had a gongong aboard that rumbled without interruption like the drums of the land army. It was to the sound of that infernal music that the ganga-ya-ita, his chief of staff and his aide-de-camp took part in the gala banquet offered by the admiral. They were served a kind of insipid broth, which the former sous-chef of the Grand Hôtel immediately baptized as "pebble soup," and a certain lake fish, the sanjika, the sovereign of intertropical waters.[9]

"Not bad, this herring," opined Isidore, "but Jack Goudron doesn't know how to make use of it. If only he's read the works of Monsieur Méry of Marseilles,[10] he'd know that this fish requires to be made into bouillabaisse."

Chocolat devoured it.

---

[9] Presumably *Opsaridium microlepsis*, the "lake salmon."

[10] An ironic reference to the Romantic writer Joseph Méry (1797-1866) who wrote several colorful novels set in various tropical regions, including Central Africa, before anything much was known about the regions in question, improvising freely.

The drums were still beating. The ganga-ya-ita, whose ears were hurting, hastened to take his leave of the admiral.

On returning to the plateau of Nyonngo, he began to inspect the land forces there without delay. The infantry troops were arranged in battle formation, but the order was singular. The lines extended in fantastic zigzags; the range of heights had been established according to the method known as "the staircase." The uniformity of the effects of costume was a mere myth. A no less successful variety reigned among the objects of armament, which seemed to have emerged pell-mell from a bric-à-brac shop. The bucklers, for example, affected circular, elliptical or hexagonal forms; they were made of cow, buffalo or rhinoceros hide; some were striped with the three colors of war, others bore red feathers, strips of white cloth and tufts of thread steeped in indigo at their perimeter.

Offensive weapons were equally various among the infantry soldiers. Some carried immeasurably long lances with goatskin pennons, others a short-handled assegai with a tip like an ace of spades. Some had small bows whose jaguar gut strings were stretched by flexible wood passed through a sheath of multicolored snakeskin; others—but not very many—had poor rifles bought by barter on the coast. There was only a certain regularity among the leaders. The captains were armed with a cazengala, the junior officers with a courbache, a long hippopotamus hide whip.

In certain respects, however, the fact of an absolute uniformity seemed uncontestable. All these effects of armament, disparate as they were, were in an equally poor state, the skins torn or holed, the wood unpolished, the iron dented. Needless to say, all the iron, intact or not, was covered by a thick layer of rust. The maintenance of weapons requires everyday care, but the Orma infantry preferred not to bother with it at all. They had ready to hand, however, the "sandpaper tree," an astonishing tree whose leaves are as rough as a tiger cat's tongue.[11] It is easy to make use of them to polish wood and metals.

The general who presented the plumed infantry troops to the Generalissimo seemed delighted by their fine turnout, but the worthy Isidore, who retained the memory of glorious times spent with the 1st zouaves, was far from sharing such an indulgent opinion.

"Oh, what wretched troopers!" he exclaimed several times. "What am I going to do with these penguins? Tell me, Mimoun, have you ever seen such specimens? But what need do I have, after all, to get queasy? They're bad, it's true, but still good enough to attack lascars who probably aren't any better. Besides which, I have numbers on my side—and what numbers! That's all I need to say. Not counting the freshwater mariners of Lake Tanganyika, I have seventy thousand men here, and seventy thousand more camping at Kifoukourou, which makes a hundred and forty thousand. Well, you see, Mimoun, when the great Clovis won the battle of Wagram, he was only at the head of thirty thousand Franks—the fruit of his economies, as Voltaire says in his *Histoire du consulat*. Well then, let's see the file-past of this host of maladroit Franks."

The file-past opened with a division of sixty beautiful elephants guided by Nubians; then the general commanding the maneuver had the infantry break into

---

[11] *Ficus exasperata*, aka the sandpaper fig—not to be confused with the American tree blessed with the same nickname.

groups, which formed up in three ranks, fifteen to twenty meters apart. Every platoon leader mounted his cow, stuffed his calumet with strong tobacco whose smoke resembled clouds of nitric acid, and strove to draw puffs whose thickness a locomotive would have envied. That done, he tranquilly set about following his men, who stretched their legs to give their rhythmic step the largest possible stride.

Smoking under arms! The new ganga-ya-ita could not get over it. He was about to get annoyed when the general informed him that the captains were merely making use of a special privilege of their rank. As for the junior officers, Isidore addressed his congratulations to them, because they were cracking their courbaches and vigorously lashing the infantrymen who were not launching themselves rapidly enough onto the warpath. They had no pity for the women of the baggage train, who were carrying enormous burdens on their heads and one or two nurslings on their backs, upright in aloe sacks. Isidore noticed that those new model service staff recognized a robust virago as their chief; she was the harpy of the previous day. Isidore recognized her at the moment when, passing in front of Mimoun, she showed him her teeth again.

"Look," said the ganga-ya-ita to his chief of staff. "That's the she-ape who was pulling faces at us yesterday when we were under the elm. She's in command of the squadron of service personnel; I think she's regretting not having been able to slice us up, because she's still pulling faces!"

The army filed past rapidly, ensigns deployed—or, to put it better, in advance of each platoon, fanatics were going crazy. There were the priest-warriors, waving crudely stuffed animal hides impaled on the ends of sticks with frenetic hands. Those astonishing ministers of the cult of the African Bellona had chosen the depictions of extremely ferocious beasts in order to throw the greatest sum of possible terror into the enemy. The heads of lions, the jaws of crocodiles, the wings of eagles and vultures were seen leaping about, while the tails of zebras floated and the coils or serpents glittered. Here and there, as if by way of a conclusion to be drawn from that phantasmagoria, scalped tresses appeared, human tibias bumping into one another, and whitened skulls whose orbits were blocked with ibis eggs.

Isidore was bewildered, astounded, and almost fearful at having to deal with pacemakers of that sort. He was allowing himself to lapse into somber reflections when one of the priest-warriors—the one who was executing, amid a thousand contortions, the most violent drum-majorish manipulations—ended up getting his legs entangled with those of his neighbor, and stumbled badly. That fall had the side effect of sending the various objects he was wearing on his head rolling to within ten paces of the stage: a bizarre assemblage of rhinoceros horns, glass beads and pink shells.

At that sight, Chocolat could not help bursting into laughter.

"Ha ha ha! The great clown's lost his hat...*bonus, bona, bonna!*"

"You never said anything so apt," said Isidore. "He's a clown, all right. We're in the middle of a carnival. A fine command I've taken on here! What a diabolical army!"

Chapter IV
Going on Campaign

At the end of the memorable review, which left him with a melancholy impression, Generalissimo Isidore nevertheless proceeded with all possible ardor with the preparations for the military operation in which he had promised to succeed. The Mata Sonapanga, this liberator of the previous day, had honored him with great confidence, and he was determined to show himself worthy of the high opinion that the young chief had of him. Nothing would have been more painful for him than to offend against the laws dictated by the sentiment of propriety.

A fortunate inspiration caused him immediately to renounce the employment of the totality of those grotesque warriors; he resolved only to employ the elite troops, if there were any. His choice settled on a thousand archers who were reputed to be the most skillful, to whom he added the men, between four and five hundred in number, who were armed with rifles. The measure was sage, but, in making it, the cook was naively changing his mind. In the morning, he had loudly proclaimed the statistics of his enormous army and praised the force of numbers; in the evening, on due reflection, he thought that two good soldiers would be worth more than twenty bad ones.

"Personally," he said, with aplomb, "I'm in favor of small, well-commanded armies, and Napoléon agreed with me! From the heights of the island of Saint Helena where the English had plunged him, he said that Turenne hadn't needed so many men to break through the Austri-

41

an lines at the Moskowa. So be it! That's why you, Mimoun, are going to look after these forty or fifty rabbits for me, organize them, mobilize them, fanaticize them, in order to make them into real soldiers. You, Chocolat, who know about vegetables, don't fail to think about the food supplies for the campaign. In every country, you see, whatever people say, it's soup that makes the soldier, as Henri II said to Sergent la Ramée."[12]

The chief of staff and the aide-de-camp immediately set to work with the most laudable zeal; Chocolat, especially, deployed an extreme activity in the execution of the prescribed service. The mission of assembling the food supplies made him smile. By that evening he had amassed a considerable quantity of rations of large red beans, potatoes and millet. The camp was overflowing with sweet potatoes, yams, manioc, sun dried fish, and small strips of meat slowly dried in termite mounds, employed by way of ovens. The expeditionary corps was provided with a host of alimentary products that the knowledgeable cook declared to be "very substantial."

"Well done!" he said to the aide-de-camp. "There are some who'd let the men go hungry, but not you—you want them to perish of indigestion."

Chocolat had not forgotten himself. Drawing a contribution from the hut containing the baggage, he had filled his supply bag with tins containing marinated tuna, lobster, salted herrings, sardines, pickles and peppers, comestibles and condiments of every kind.

Having completed their tasks, Mimoun and Chocolat hastened to inform their commanding general

---

[12] "Sergent la Ramée" [approximately, Sergeant Evergreen] was a standard personification of a French soldier, often featured in cartoons and numerous comic literary works.

that, in conformity with his orders, everything was ready; that absolutely nothing as lacking, not even a gaiter button—for the simple reason that the Orma warriors went barefoot. The sun was setting in the Tanganyika; Isidore fixed the time of departure for daybreak the following day.

The next day, therefore, Chocolat had the food supplies and all of the general staff's baggage loaded onto the backs of female porters under the command of the sorceress, whom Isidore nicknamed the Tringlote.[13]

That done, the column set forth.

The ganga-ya-ita was mounted on Moonchild, Mimoun on his black and white cow. Chocolat followed, gravely sitting astride his donkey; his feet were trailing on the ground and his supply bag was making pronounced metallic clinking sounds.

The expeditionary force headed directly for the camp at Kifoukourou, established three days march to the north of the Nyonngo plateau. First they had to pass through a few villages whose inhabitants had abandoned them, but which were still surrounded by magnificent gardens. Pineapples, fig, dates, oranges and even grapes were to be found there. The fields adjacent to those orchards offered a no less splendid aspect. Maize could be seen there, imported from Europe, manioc imported from America, sugar cane imported from southern Asia, and crops of all kinds: millet, rice, coffee, cotton, madder and indigo. Isidore marveled at so much wealth. Mimoun murmured, sententiously: "He who puts his confidence in God lives amid the goods of the world."

---

[13] A slang term for female military service staff, or, more disdainfully, camp followers.

Chocolat stuffed himself with figs and oranges, and did so with no other preoccupation.

They then had to cut across, perpendicular to its thalweg, the dry bed of a stream snaking through an opulent savannah covered with thick grass more than two and a half meters high. The column disappeared entirely for a while into that vegetal thicket, in which grasses and leguminous plants were dominant. As for the banks of the dry stream, they were shaded by date palms, doum palms, pandana palms, baobabs, orchids and passion flowers. Lianas formed superb garlands, running from one tree to the next and enlacing them together like serpents. A little further on, it was necessary to ford several small fast-flowing watercourses, tributaries of the Tanganyika.

Eventually, they stopped, in order to rest, on the bank of a small pond whose troubled waters were the color of a cup of black tea—a shade resulting from the infusion of dead leaves. It was about nine o'clock in the morning.

The prairie in which the pond was located almost exactly in the center was delightful in appearance; it was a true garden, marvelously planted with beautiful plants; mimosas, banana trees, fig trees, palm trees, coconut palms, acacias and sycamores formed leafy groves where grass grew in mammoth lumps three or four meters high. Unfortunately, however, that charming paradise gave shelter to mysterious bloodthirsty insects.

The entomological fauna there had representatives of all species. One could see flying coleoptera, like the goliath beetle and the bucephalus stag beetle; legions of black ants and white ants were swarming; long columns of red ants were going to war; caterpillars were raining down; innumerable hosts of earwigs were racing in all directions. One could hear the drone of yellow-headed wasps the size of hummingbirds and the whine of cock-chafers the size of sparrows; vermin of every sort could be felt wriggling, which a microscope would not have failed to translate into apocalyptic monsters armed with pincers, lances, suckers and darts as terrible as those of our black hussars and all the aptera of old Europe. In Africa, it is absolutely necessary to renounce killing those implacable enemies and resign oneself to letting them die of indigestion on one's skin.

The preparations for the torture promised to the travelers were sung in prelude by a frightful humming. One kind of fly, which can be distinguished by its low-pitched voice, measures no less than three centimeters in length; it is the horse fly of Central Africa. Another, which sings contralto in the terrible concert, is well known for its indomitable malevolence, its inextinguishable thirst for blood. A kind of winged ant about two and a half centimeters long, it is named the *tsetse*, by virtue of a facile onomatopoeia, the mere hearing of which never fails to cast a certain chill into the conversation of European voyagers.

And the name tsetse is not yet the last word of the tortures that await the passage of explorers of the African continent. Of all the equatorial mosquitoes, the one reputed to be the most vicious is the *insondo*, which takes the tenor role and sounds the brass instruments. That ferocious little beast introduces itself into the trunk of an elephant, which it easily drives into a fury; it is fond of the epidermis of negroes; its sting is often mortal.

In addition, the edges of the charming little pond offered all the characteristics of spume, spongy ground into which one sinks, causing bubbles to emerge at every step that burst on the surfaces of the mud and exhale odors of hydrogen sulfide. The previous night, a penetrating mist had settled over the surface of the pool, which was gradually allowing itself to be torn apart by the sun's already-ardent rays. Under the influence of the warm humidity of the African climate, which the inflexible Isidore characterized as "torrential heat," wood rots, metal oxidize, garments become soaked, gunpowder disintegrates, leather passes into a gelatinous state and cardboard is liquefied…and the human organism can take its choice between hypertrophy of the thyroid gland and the dysentery of elephantiasis.

Isidore had not forgotten the bitter taste of the quinine sulfate that the physician-major of the zouaves had once given him, nor the diagnosis—nowadays vulgarized—of the circumstances than can engender malarial fever. Beneath the cheerful aspect of a beautiful scene of luxuriant vegetation he sniffed insalubrity, and hastened to declare that they had better get under way after a few minutes' rest. The Orma infantry, far from lying down, took advantage of the brief halt to run after the files of white ants that were fleeing through the grass. They guzzled them as if they were strawberries; they constitute a delicacy, a refreshment much appreciated by the populations of central Africa.

Having resumed its march, the column arrived at the foot of a hill at about four o'clock, the slope of which it climbed. At the summit, the air was fresh and pure, free of any miasma; furthermore, one of the slopes was modeled in such a fashion that there was hope of finding water there at a shallow depth. It was immediately decided that they would spend the night in that delightful spot, known in the region by the name of Ougogo.

The steward, Chocolat, rapidly dug a well. Having also taken care to make the Tringlote's women carry a sufficient number of hand mills, he proceeded with a distribution of millet. Every man ground his own ration, dampened the flour obtained in order to make a syrupy broth, divided that pulp into balls rounded out on the palm of the hand, and finally dined lavishly.

After a good night's sleep, they resumed the march in the direction of Kifoukourou.

"Move off, wretched troop!" Isidore had said. "Messieurs courbache-sergeants, I recommend the laggards to you. We haven't finished the difficult part of our journey; it even appears that it might get harder."

In fact, the northern slope of the hill of Ougogo descended onto an arid plain—or, rather, a dried-up marsh of which the spongy ground had formed a black soil more than a meter thick resting on a bed of river sand. The plain was strewn with shells and small mounds or clod of earth similar to those that moles make, but the size of a top hat. That multitude of tumescences, the subterranean work of crabs, made the walking very difficult for the infantrymen, who also had to be careful not to step on small venomous snakes that were wriggling here and there on the burning surface of the sand.

To cap it all, there was nothing to eat in that desert plain, which was absolutely bare. At about half past ten, a few Ormas, tormented by hunger, took various items of food from the depths of their quivers, which they had prudently kept in reserve. Each of them ate a ball about the size of a lady apple, assuring the steward Chocolat that on that nourishment alone they could support several days of fatigue, and even combats—which the worthy jack-jack permitted himself to doubt. As for the master cook Isidore, the degustation was quickly accomplished, in order to demonstrate to him that the paste of the extraordinary balls was made of butter and coffee mixed in such proportions that it resulted in a sufficiently great consistency.

Not all the men were provided with such a reserve of alimentary paste, however, and they were preparing to make a distribution of food taken from the supplies to the column when the sky was suddenly obscured. A thick cloud was passing over the Ormas' heads, and they began uttering loud cries of delight.

"Gangas! Gangas! Gangas!" they shouted.

It was, indeed, and enormous swarm of *gangas*, or Biblical quail—which is to say, of the same the species as those that once served to nourish Moses' Hebrews, also known as desert partridges. It was those birds, very widespread in equatorial latitudes, which gave the African continent its ancient name of Ortygia.[14]

The cloud was skimming the ground. It was not difficult to bring down a number of them, struck with stones or even sticks. The troops had enough to make a good meal. Thus restored, they resumed marching and made light work of the afternoon stage. That evening, they took shelter at the edge of the beautiful forest of Ougaga.

Myriads of birds already perched in the high branches greeted the red light of the setting sun with their chirping. Within the noisy concert the particular songs could be distinguished as a crowd of various per-

---

[14] The Greek *Ortyx* means quail, and that meaning gives the present Greek island of Ortygia its name via a myth of metamorphosis. The name was also given by the Greeks to several other places, although I can find no evidence that one of them was the African continent.

formers: secretary birds, bee-eaters, kingfishers, grosbeaks, hummingbirds in metallic colors. The intervals were punctuated by the piercing cries emitted by the shrike, the whydah, the barbican, the coucal, the trogon, the bustard and a multitude of other soloists with shrill or deep voices. The ensemble had for accompaniment the cooing of ringdoves, the clicking beaks of storks, the tonal modulations of hammerkops, crab plovers and wood ibis.

Night fell; all the birds fell silent. Familiar voices imposed silence on them: those of monkeys yapping in chorus before going to sleep. The cries could easily be made out of the dog-faced baboon, the gorilla or soko, the bald-headed man of the woods, which builds its huts in the summits of tall baobabs.[15]

Those braying quadrumanes did not threaten to trouble the repose of the expeditionary corps; on the other hand, however, there was some danger of attack by wild beasts. Big cats are abundant in the region of the lakes; so, in order to protect his people from any serious danger, the prudent Isidore had fires lit on the edge of the forest that would be maintained all night long.

At daybreak, the camp was lifted in order to traverse the forest of Ougaga, which crowns the heights profiled in sharp-toothed sierras. When they had emerged

---

[15] The taxonomy of the primates was still confused in the mid-19th century, the situation not having been helped in the least by the Comte de Buffon, whose supposedly-definitive *Histoire naturelle* had mixed up chimpanzees, gorillas and orangutans on the basis of inaccurate traveler's tales, much as the author does here (*soko* being an African term for chimpanzee). It was Buffon who dubbed the great apes "quadrumanes," meaning four-handed.

from its thickets and it was necessary to begin descending the northern slopes of the chain, they perceived that a great obstacle would soon oppose forward progress: the feet of the wooded heights were bathed in water. A considerable flood extended where the column's guides thought they would find an easy and reliable route. The soil was drowned by an expanse of water whose breadth it was impossible to calculate.

Such inundations are not uncommon in intertropical Africa, where rivers, when they flood, often cover thirty or forty kilometers of the plain to either side of their beds. The lands thus occupied were already occupied by numerous aquatic populations: crowned cranes, demoiselle cranes, ibis, purple swamp hens, guinea fowl, pelicans and ducks. The edges of the new lake region were sparkling in the sunlight; they were radiant with long streaks of dazzling whiteness. Those silvery ribbons were mirror-bright; they were simply schools of fresh water fish, which, cast out of their habitual dwellings by the flood and left to dry out in the hot sun, were searching for a new homeland as best they could. Fluvial overflows frequently give rise to such migrations of the scaly folk; fish have known to cross four or five kilometers of land nose-to-tail in quest of the liquid element in which to re-immerse themselves.

Meanwhile, the ganga-ya-ita Isidore was wondering how he could reckon with this obstacle. Wade through it? There was no possibility of that. They would have had water up to their thighs, or perhaps their waists; they would have had to splash though mud, slipping at every step and risking falling into potholes. There were also other dangers no less serious to run. A slow-flowing river seemed to have been diverted from its usual bed, fraying a new course through the flood water, and that river was already inhabited by troops of alligators that were bellowing like bulls.

"*Gaymanos*, Señor Isidore," murmured Chocolat, sadly. "*Gaymanos* always hungry! *Libera nos a malo*, Cacuaco."

"Diabolical river!" exclaimed the guides, no longer knowing what route the column ought to follow.

"Bad tobacco," said the zouave into Mimoun's ear. "Bad tobacco! How are we going to get out of this?"

"*Ouatsoq bi Allah*!" murmured the Muslim—trust in God.[16]

The penetrating eyesight of the worthy spahi, habituated since childhood to the rapid reconnaissance of the most obscure horizons, had already perceived in the distance a practical path emerging from the flood water, like the stout cable of a rescue anchor. He indicated clearly, in an easterly direction, a verdant mass that cut through the expanse of the tumultuous waters. The object that he pointed out to Isidore was not an island circled by two branches of the river but a *sinndi* or continuous raft floating from one bank to the other.

Such sinndis are not made by human hands; nature alone takes the trouble. Swollen by diluvian rains, the waters ferry thick tangles of uprooted trunks, broken branches and plants torn up by the wind. Aquatic weeds and lianas carried away by the current suffice to provide cumulative frameworks as they become entangled with the debris, and the natural rafts that result from the aggregations can serve for the passage of heavy caravans.

---

[16] The formulation *ouatsoq bi allah* is given in a dictionary of the Algerian language published by Théodore de Bussy in 1838, from which the author presumably took it. The modern equivalent would probably be *Tawakkaltu ala Allah*.

It is one of the curiosities of the African continent, so rich in marvels of every sort.

Following Mimoun's precious indications, therefore, they headed eastwards until they reached the desired point. There they found another marvel. Human industry, the ever-present parasite, had already set up home on one of the ends of the recently-born raft. Scarcely had it emerged from the hand of Mother Nature when the sinndi had been monopolized by a "lord of the waters," a ridiculous tyrant who had arrogated the right to impose an exorbitant toll on travelers. Needless to say, the inane lord refrained from annoying the ganga-ya-ita of the army of the great Mata Sonapanga!

Isidore had the means of passage that the wooden train offered his column carefully reconnoitered. It was tested from one end to the other with all the customary precautions; then the troop was broken up into a number of smaller groups, which received orders to file across the floating causeway, but only one after another.

Finally, the fifteen hundred men passed over.

Delighted with his success, Isidore could not restrain himself from complimenting the clear-sighted Mimoun cheerfully.

"You really are the cleverest explorer I ever met," he said. "What you've just done, you see, is better than Moses departing for Syria, because, after all, we passed over with dry feet, while a little water remained in the Black Sea for Moses. Even King Pharamond swallowed a few mouthfuls there. Now, let's be on our way! Let's get our legs moving! When one marches, one covers the ground, and in the evening one reaches the camp site—isn't that so, Mimoun?"

"*Insha'Allah!*" replied the pious spahi—if God wills it.

The detour made by the column in order to cross the sinndi had taken considerable time, and it was pitch dark by the time they reached the lines of the army corps of seventy thousand men forming the blockade of Kisimbasimba. The general quarters of the corps was established in a village named Kifoukourou. There, as in the camp at Nyonngo, the besieging troops were partly camped in bomas and partly gathered in defensive hamlets. They hardly ever emerged from their lines, following the principle they had adopted of blockading the enemy by way of a continuous din.

The former zouave drummer began by instructing all the gongongs to quiet. Then he placed sentries at some distance from the place, whose ramparts were profiled vaguely in the gloom, and went to camp in front of Kifoukourou, on a sandy hillock sown with clumps of jujube trees. He had his reasons for doing that; he did not want his elite troops to come into contact with the incompetents of the besieging troop.

They went to bed, but the ganga-ya-ita slept badly. All night long, he never ceased to experience strange sensations in his skin, unfamiliar pricklings, perhaps due to the swarming of an army of ungraspable entities.

When he got up he was not surprised to see his men dispersed in the fields. The worthy fellows were hunting, like pure gentlemen, except that what they were hunting were little mice that were wriggling there in multitudes. And what were they doing with them? Eating them!

Antiquity was familiar with the struthiophages, or ostrich-eaters, the ichthyophages, who lived on fish, and the acridophages, who nourished themselves on locusts; Isidore had before his eyes myophages, or eaters of field mice.

At the sight of the black men swallowing the little rodents as people in France swallow pills, Chocolat could not suppress a gesture of disgust. As he, too, was hungry, however, he took a can of sardines out of his supply bag, opened it with the aid of his big knife, and briskly transferred the contents to his stomach.

The ganga-ya-ita was in haste to proceed with the operation of the attack; he gathered his men to make them take up arms.

Since the previous day, however, the armaments had suffered grave degradations; the bows and quivers, the butts of the rifles, belts and cartridge cases were out of action.

The mice had chewed up everything!

Chapter VI
He Who Scratches Here Gets Stung

"No luck!" said Isidore. "I'm no more a fool than the next man, but truly, this hasn't begun well. There's no time to lose, though. I promised that young man to settle this little business in two days; it's absolutely necessary that it ends today or tomorrow. Go on, Mimoun, reorganize that detachment of imbeciles who let their effects get eaten. Have them replace what they've lost— borrow weapons from the blockading troops who were beating their drums yesterday evening for fear of spirits! We're not as frivolous."

While the faithful Mimoun went to collect the equipment necessary to the conquest from the bomas and hamlets of the lines, the commanding general mounted Moonchild and left the bivouac at Kifoukourou in order to go and carry out a regulation reconnaissance. At the advance posts he observed that the Ormas of the besieging army had suspended from the branches of all the trees a bizarre assemblage of passably disparate objects, to wit: a corncob, an arrow and a cockerel's feather. He learned that this rebus signified a declaration of war to the death on the people of Kisimbasimba.

Beyond that line of bellicose emblems, the ganga-ya-ita was easily able to convince himself that the defenses of the location comprised at least two enclosures: an initial envelope or latticework palisade; and a second timber stockade made of horizontally-laid tree trunks. A rather deep ditch opened in between the two. What was behind the stockade? Impossible to determine, for, doubtless slotted together in groves like pieces of carpentry, the wood opposed an impenetrable barrier to the eye. From the height of his ambulant observatory, Isidore could not succeed in looking any further into the interior. No sound emerged from behind the ramparts; the silence was absolute. Was the singular city deserted then, as the Ormas claimed?

Bah! What are these stories? The imperturbable cook said to himself. *Stupidities! We'll see about that. There's someone lurking behind that barrier, I'm sure, like a hare that has a presentiment of the jug, and that scent isn't telling him any lie; he's going to die! Just wait a little, my rabbits!*

When Isidore got down from Moonchild, his resolutions were made; he had frankly adopted the method of attack by intimidation. It ought to be said that for two years he had never seen any other method than that one put into practice, and that it had always succeeded fully. In Africa, in fact, the natives have a great fear of firearms. If a band of brigands surrounds a village and fires a few rifle shots at the perimeter of the palisade, the fearful inhabitants immediately surrender, beg for mercy, and allow themselves to be captured. That was how the *Mazitous*—a predatory people who were then desolating the region of the lakes—operated; it was thus that a scoundrel by the name of Kisabengo had succeeded in striking terror into five or six large provinces; and that a certain Mchiri, at the head of a few rascally Ounyamouesi had conquered the kingdom of Katanga, west of Tanganyika, at very little expense.[17]

---

[17] These details—and, indeed, many of the previous details of Isidore's journey and the accompanying comments—are taken

Isidore sent forth a hundred men, re-armed thanks to Mimoun, deployed them in a chain of riflemen a few paces from the latticework palisade, and ordered them to begin the attack immediately by carrying out a sustained indirect fire over the wall formed by the inner stockade.

An allegro movement, however, was scarcely in harmony with the character of those elite men. Without hurrying, they started brandishing their weapons, snarling like wild beasts, rolling their eyes in such a way that only the whites could be seen, and singing death songs. Finally, they started dancing like bears. They set out to imitate the animal, copying it as slavishly as possible. They leapt about, beating the air with their arms, simultaneously shouting, yelping and howling. After ten minutes of that violent exercise, they were enthused. Their junior officers, judging that they were ready, drove them with whiplashes to the positions that they were to occupy in order to launch the impending action.

"Diabolical troopers!" exclaimed Isidore, bewildered. "Have you ever seen such a fantasia, Mimoun?"

"*Mahbout besefe!*" said the chief of the general staff—they're insane.

"Finally, they're at their posts! That's fortunate. Let's go—commence firing, riflemen! And you, archers, try to clear the stockade!"

Lively musket fire was heard; the top of the timber stockade was peppered by a hail of projectiles: deformed bullets cut out of lead sheets and rolled by hand, and arrows with iron tips fitted into fish bones and fletched with toucan feathers.

---

from Henry Morton Stanley's memoir *How I Found Livingstone in Central Africa* (1872)

The Orma archers are reputed to be the most skillful in the entire continent, and it is certain that they make rapid fire a genuine specialty. It is said that they are able to fire twenty-eight arrows consecutively, and that the twenty-eighth would quit the bow before the first had fallen to earth. The reputation seems to be well merited, allowing for the exaggeration that must be credited to central African reporters. Following the principles of their national tactics, each of the Ormas swiftly launched a salvo of arrows, and, in order to ward off the adversary's riposte, immediately whirled his hatchet around his head; then he unleashed another salvo...and so on.

The defenders made no response.

Isidore ordered a second attack, and then a third.

The besieged gave no sign of life: still the same inertia, the same immobility, the same silence.

"Is there no one there?" said the ganga-ya-ita. "Come on, show yourselves—we won't do you any harm."

Only the echoes replied to Isidore's voice.

"Come on," he said. "No one's budging. That's all right—we'll get there another way. In the meantime, let's not throw our powder to the sparrows. Cease fire!"

While Isidore was thinking about making other arrangements, the riflemen and the archer did not hesitate to sing a victory song—an exorbitant pretention in itself, but which did no harm to anyone. They uttered the cry of delight: "Lou! Lou! Lou! Lou! Lou! Lou!"—a cry that has no other inconvenience than that of not advancing matters an inch.

Isidore told them to shut up, and, having gathered them in a fold in the terrain, instructed them not to move. Mimoun was charged with making sure that the order was rigorously obeyed. While the victors ruminated their cries of delight, the former zouave drummer, accompanied by Chocolat, moved stealthily to the foot of the palisade. There, taking his aide-de-camp's hatchet, he launched a forceful blow at the obstacle in order to test its strength.

"It's hard wood," he said. "Impossible to cut through, but we'll reckon with it, or I'll lose your Latin in the process."

He began cutting through the wadding of lianas that linked the palings together; once isolated, the latter became vulnerable. The two men set about rocking one of them within its slot; after a few backward and forward movements they succeeded in uprooting it. That was the most difficult one. By means of the same procedure they extracted a second and a third, and eventually had a breach large enough to give passage to a column of men eight or ten abreast.

That done, the commanding general dispatched his aide-de-camp Chocolat to Mimoun, to tell him to bring up all his men to positions at the open palisade, in order to support from there the workers charged with going to open a similar breach in the inner stockade.

A few moments later, Mimoun arrived at the indicated point. His men were gathered to either side of the passage opened in the palisade, ready to move forward at the first signal.

Scarcely had they occupied that new position, however, when a great tumult rose up among them, soon followed by a greater disorder. They were no longer giving any thought to singing. The "Lou! Lou! Lou!" had caught in their throats. That was because a host of extraordinary projectiles was raining down upon them, including flaming darts, copper ingots in the form of St. Andrew's crosses, fragments of the shafts of columns more than half a cubic meter in diameter, granite statuettes, marble sphinxes, and terra-cotta vases of the most elegant design, recalling that of the amphora of the Villa Diomedes in Pompeii—but which, on shattering into a thousand pieces on the ground released multitudes of hungry rats, or venomous snakes with mortal bites.

The Ormas were devastated. For them, these various projectiles, manufactured in the arsenals of the heavens, could only have been launched by the invisible hand of the satanic Loubari, or Moussa, the evil spirit that floats on the waters of Lake Tanganyika—or even, some said, the little demon named Moussamouira, haunting the places where the mice had nibbled the armaments. That little spirit had doubtless been woken up by the evil eye with which Chocolat, the lanky individual with the yellow skin who was the ganga-ya-ita's courtier, was afflicted.

As for Isidore, he was amazed. He had every right to be astonished to see stones of such caliber falling, stones of a size large enough to crush an elephant. On observing the trajectories, however, he became convinced that they were departing from various points situated immediately behind the stockade.

"I was certain of it," he said, with self-satisfaction. "The city isn't abandoned. There's someone in there, behind that wooden wall. To the two of us, Messieurs! Mimoun, arrange your men in a single line, right up against the palisade; that way, there's no danger for them. Above all, use the courbache well, so that your rabbits don't run away!"

Having said that, Isidore, still followed by Chocolat, threw himself bravely forward into the gap between the palisade and the wall, leaping into the ditch.

His old zouave's glance has not deceived him; the enemy fire is following a curved trajectory; the projectiles, passing over his head, cannot reach him.

On his order, Chocolat starts briskly cutting the brushwood growing in the ditch. The general sets an example to his aide-de-camp; the two of them compete in ardor, tearing up desiccated plants, piling up dead branches and assembling anything combustible that comes to hand. They make torches of them by binding them with lianas, clamber up the side of the ditch, and transport their bundles of flammable material one by one to the foot of the obstacle.

There they set fire to them.

Thick smoke envelops the stockade; then flames appear and start licking the logs. The conflagration bursts forth, the wood crackles. In a matter of minutes, the logs will be reduced to ashes.

Isidore, who has rejoined Mimoun, then gives the signal for the assault in a curt tone. The Ormas form a column as best they can, crossing the breach in the palisade and then the ditch. They arrive at the stockade, where the breach, although still smoking, is already practicable.

Instead of precipitating themselves into it, the excited warriors start uttering their eternal "Lou! Lou! Lou!" and launch themselves into their insensate pyrrhic dance. The black forms outlined against the backcloth of the final flames of the blaze remind Isidore of an old picture in the church of Six-Fours representing groups of the damned sketching out a macabre dance on the Day of the Dead in front of the gate of Hell.

"Decidedly," he said, "I have a rude detachment there! Diabolical soldiers who are afraid of passing through the fire! Has anyone ever seen such a thing?"

Suddenly, the scene changes. The assault column designs undulations and singular eddies. Solutions of continuity are manifest. The unfortunate column begins to break up and has soon disintegrated. The warriors who were dancing and calculating the pleasures of triumph a few moments before shamelessly turn their backs to the retrenchment, assuming the most pitiful attitudes and howling at the top of their voices a great cry of distress: "Eyah! Eyah! Eyah! Eyah! Eyah! Eyah!"

Some apply their hands to their faces, other to their bellies; some are writhing, as if gripped by colic, others are rolling on the ground and moaning. They all seem grotesquely confused.

The assault column has just been assailed by legions of bees: the African bees whose rage Schweinfurth and Stanley have described for us.[18] Astonishingly, those ferocious swarms are emerging from the stockade; they are vomiting forth from the breach!

""Truly, I have no luck at all!" exclaims the ganga-ya-ita, for the second time. "It's not good here, eh! The great philosophers were right to say that those who scratch...isn't that right, Chocolat?"

But Chocolat did not hear his general. In the midst of the panic, he had paused at the bottom of the ditch, and there, calmly, he was opening another tin of sardines with his large knife.

---

[18] Georg August Schweinfurth's *Im Herzen von Afrika* (1874; tr. as *The Heart of Africa*) was presumably another of the sources on which the author drew in researching his novel.

Chapter VII
The Moment to Open Fire

All the Orma riflemen, stung to the quick, had executed a burlesque retreat. They got back to Kifoukourou in the most lamentable state, proclaiming loudly that rather than ferocious insects they would have preferred to confront the fury of a herd of buffalo or a troop of lions. That was undoubtedly hyperbole, but it is affirmed that the stings of African bees are capable of causing painful lesions that rapidly throw the human organism into grave disorder. In spite of the thickness of his dermis, the negro cannot escape the effects of ulceration; his limbs are tumefied, his face swells up, and the wounded man does not take long to die in convulsions.

Only Chocolat had escaped unscathed—and the Ormas claimed that the tall deadpan humorist had the evil eye, that he bore on his forehead the imprint of the devil's finger, that he had made a pact with the Spirits of the Lake, that the traitor had been able to unleash the winged folk upon his companions in arms, while having, of course, the ability to preserve himself personally from their assaults.

Mimoun had bravely shared the common fate; his skin color had passed from black to violet-tinged red; his cheeks were streaked with bright red and violet veins.

Isidore had not escaped the action of the sharp darts of the enraged little creatures either. The tumefaction of his cheeks had taken on the proportions of a Neapolitan *cocomero* melon, and his nose the form of a pineapple. He was unrecognizable when he was obliged to interfere in order to prevent anyone doing harm to his aide-de-camp. On the other hand, furious at such a check, astounded by the bad luck that had prevented his magnificent military schemes from succeeding, he could not dissimulate his murderous mood when, on re-entering the lines, he suddenly found himself face to face with the Mata Sonapanga. For a poor white ganga-ya-ita, miserably driven back by a swarm of honey-flies, the encounter could only be disagreeable.

"Mousoungou," said the Mata Sonapanga, allowing his paired eyebrows to describe violent circumflex accents, "Mousoungou, I have followed in your footsteps; I came to sing with you the song of victory, to raise you up on our sacred elephant, to exchange blood with you as a sign of eternal amity. You promised me to take Kisimbasimba. What are you doing? Is your promise no more than a joke? Why have you not taken the banza?"

"Young man," said Isidore, "do you think this is comfortable? I've had a setback. I've been unlucky."

"Ouaka had inspired me; I thought you were a genius."

"Genius, me? No—I've served in the zouaves, but don't be silly. Come on, young man, let's be just, but honest. It's necessary to be reasonable. I promised you to have that city, and I asked you for two days, which isn't excessive! Today is only the first day, and it isn't finished yet. Well, I'm no longer asking you for anything but the rest of today. One can't be more modest than that. This morning, the battle was lost, it's true, but it's only two o'clock or quarter past. We have time to win another, as Turenne said to the grenadier guards. You see, young man, let me do things my way; you're a great Mata, but I'm clever. This morning, we got stung, that's true, but we also made a hole in the fortifications;

one can pass through it easily, and soon, you'll see, it will be the moment to open fire. Now, I'm only asking you for ten minutes' rest—because, in truth, I can no longer see; my nose is getting into my eyes."

The Mata Sonapanga had the good faith to recognize the justice of the ganga-ya-ita's observations. In consequence, he hastened to have cares lavished upon him. On his orders, the chief of military physicians applied a palliative cataplasm to his face; at the same time, the Tringlote brought the wounded a cordial capable of waking the dead. It was a beverage composed of sesame oil infused with *bamia* flowers, aloe leaves and peppers previously permeated with salts of soda.

Isidore moistened his lips in the straw goblet that was presented to him. Immediately, his hair stood on end. Compared with that drug, Madame Gibou's famous tea[19] could pass for orgeat syrup. Retrenching himself intelligently behind the prohibitions of Muslim law, Mimoun firmly resisted the invitation of the long-toothed Tringlote; he refused to drink even a single drop of the infidel wine.

As for Chocolat, who always did what people wanted of him, he casually drank a few mouthfuls, which did not even make him blink. With a blissful smile, he declared: "*Manducaverum* of sardines; *bibi* of cocoa; *bono!*"

After an hour's rest, Isidore declared that it was time to take up the thread of the interrupted operations. He got everyone on their feet, climbed onto Moonchild, and prepared to cross the gap of five or six hundred me-

---

[19] In the famous farce by Théophile Dumersan, *Madame Gibou et Madame Pochet, ou le Thé chez la ravaudeuse* (1832).

ters between the besiegers' lines and the city's defenses. He arranged his men in a tight column with a front as wide as the breaches, and made them move at the double, threatening anyone who made as if to break ranks with the courbache.

And they set off on the warpath once again.

Eighty meters from the latticework palisade, the general let his troops take a breather; then he ordered the charge, in order to pour through the breach like a torrent between the piles of a bridge. He thought that by virtue of the acquired momentum, they would pass over the ditch swiftly; mentally, he calculated the force of the shock by multiplying the mass by the velocity, and concluded that they would arrive at the stockade in excellent conditions to drive back the defenders of the breach. That would then be the moment to open fire and to bring the affair to a conclusion.

Such was Isidore's plan.

Following that plan, he launches his attack column forward. They arrive at the palisade—but what do they encounter there? One of those snags that the Americans call "diabolical surprises." The breach is obstructed, and by what? By a row of enchained buffaloes, tightly packed together, forming a barricade, heads lowered, presenting their long horns to the aggressors.

"Forward!" cried the excited Isidore. "Forward!"

With that, the commanding general, bravely setting an example, gets down from Moonchild, unsheathes his large hussar's saber and promptly stabs a first buffalo, and then a second—but at the third thrust, the long blade breaks on one of the chosen victim's bones. The splinters of iron, projected in a spray, nearly put out Isidore's eyes. He no longer has anything in his hand but a hilt without a blade.

"Wooden sword!" he says, throwing the debris away. "Truly, I have no luck at all—but that's all right; one can carry on; let's carry on. Forward! Forward!"

With Mimoun having enlarged the breach by felling three more beasts with revolver shots, the column resumes its course as best it can, crossing the pass and reforming under cover in the bottom of the ditch. From there, the stockade is only one step away.

The general gives the signal for the attack; everyone launches forward, scaling the wall; they arrive at the breach opened by the morning's fire.

"Let's go!" says Isidore, somewhat reassured. "This time, it will go like clockwork. Come on, a little courage! Forward, friend! Forward, forward!"

But the friends are hanging back. They seem hesitant, swooning with terror. Finally, they prostrate themselves, in conformity with the customs of the region, muttering bizarre litanies.

"*Ganga nzumba! Nzumba djoudou...! Ganga nzumba...!*"—and so on, indefinitely, without advancing by a single step, or making any movement at all.

Isidore no longer understands anything. What can be happening now?

Briefly, Mimoun reveals the seemingly mysterious causes of this new disarray. Among the Ormas, the he-goat is a sacred animal; it is the god of battles, the living idol of war. No one dares touch it, or even to look at it; one renders it divine honors; it is essentially *djoudou*— which is to say, inviolable. Anyone who does not fear to confront the sight of one is profane.

Now, in the breadth of the breach, three he-goats with long white beards are attached to stakes planted in the ground.

"Oh!" said Isidore, utterly disconcerted. "I've seen a lot of things in my life, but I've never had such cardboard soldiers under my nose. Mimoun, take care of this for me."

The chief of the general staff detached the goats rapidly—which, turning round, departed at top speed for the interior of the besieged location.

The way was clear.

"Let's go, lads!" cried Isidore. "Look lively! On your feet! The goats have gone! The moment has come to open fire; we're about to take the banza! And it's not some wretched village; it's a banza greater than Constantinople, one of the greatest capitals of China. The city's ours. Forward, lads, forward!"

But the lads did not move.

"Come on!" Isidore went on, already very annoyed. "A little courage! The sun's setting—this is the moment to open fire!"

No one budged.

Along the lines, however, confused noises rose up. A concert of lamentable voices was heard, and, as the tumult increased, the members of the attack column, still lying on the ground, were soon able to make out the meaning of the cries uttered in the advance posts of the Kifoukourou lines: "*Eya! Eya! Motto! Motto!*"

What was happening, then? At the moment so well determined by Isidore for opening fire, it was fire that was taking hold behind him, propagating rapidly through the dry grass, threatening to set everything ablaze.

The piercing cries encountered echoes in the attack column. Without paying any further heed to whether or not to render themselves culpable of sacrilegious gazes, the pious warriors rose to their feet, shouting in their turn: "*Motto! Motto! Motto!*"

The peril was great. To ward it off, there was no time to lose.

Stopped in front by the place where his men have refused to set foot, Isidore sees that he is being attacked from the rear by the conflagration. He orders the retreat, cursing his eternal bad luck.

They go back through the palisade, which will probably soon burn down. Beyond it, they perceive fires wandering through the vicinity. Everything is burning. Lianas are writhing, wood is spitting; it is a sea of flame! And all the Ormas flee recklessly, shouting: "Bush fire! Bush fire!"

Isidore climbs back on to Moonchild in order to get out of the circle of fire. The brave beast sets off at her rapid amble, but suddenly makes an abrupt lurch. The ganga-ya-ita is nearly thrown overboard.

"Hey!" says Isidore. "My mount seems to be pitching. What's up?"

"Simba! Simba!" replies the mahout.

A lion, uttering frightful roars, has hurled itself forward to attack the elephant, but the latter, having, so to speak, caught it on the wing and wrapped her trunk around it, has just crushed it underfoot—hence the lurch.

"There, Matoto, there!" says the Hindu, caressing the beast.

"Another Simba!" says Mimoun, a moment later.

Another furious lion has attacked his elephant from behind and lacerated her with its teeth.

Unsaddled, Mimoun beat a retreat toward his general, who extended the ladder for him. From the height of the haoussah, the hunter hastened to fire at the wild beast, which fell dead. He then pointed out to Isidore that the beast had no tail, and that the said appendage had been recently cut off. He was explaining that the ablation had probably been carried out in Kisimbasimba, and that the lion had emerged from the besieged location, when shrill screams rang out, uttered by Chocolat, whose terrified little donkey had just taken refuge under the elephant's belly.

"The lion, Señor Isidore! The lion seeking *quem decoret...*!"

Indeed, a third lion was racing forward at top speed. Blood was spurting from the root of its severed tail.

Formed as he was like a wading bird, the mulatto had no need of a ladder. He held out his long arms to Isidore, who grabbed his hands and hauled him up onto the haoussah. The aide-de-camp, like the chief of staff, was saved. This time, kneeling down, he rendered thanks to San José de Cacuaco, whose protecting hand he recognized.

Mimoun, shooting the lion, saved the little gray donkey—but it was not over.

Other lions were arriving from all directions, like bands of skirmishers, pursuing the Orma infantrymen, overtaking the fugitives or leaving them no other escape route than to plunge into the flames.

Mimoun fired from the elephant's back in vain; scarcely had he put one animal down when another beast appeared to replace the fallen comrade. The lions, which were running furiously, were all devoid of a tail, and blood was dripping from their wound. Mimoun ran out of cartridges.

They were still in the midst of the fires, which it was necessary to get through as soon as possible, under threat of being roasted alive.

The situation, which had become desperate, was fortunately saved by Moonchild. The brave animal, whose mahout had abandoned her to the inspirations of an instinct comparable to human intelligence, discovered a tongue of land, an isthmus that the flames had not yet reached. She precipitated her amble in the required direction, and, thanks to the vivacity of her stride, passed through the fjord framed by two blazes.

She was just in time.

The travelers in the haoussah had scarcely come through the pass when the flames closed the circle behind them.

"Well," said Isidore, "do I have bad luck! As misfortune goes, that's misfortune, or I don't know myself. It's complete!"

The cook was mistaken; his disaster was yet to have a completion; he was about to drink the cup of bitterness to the dregs.

Chapter VIII
Sack and Rope.

The first human face that the unfortunate cook encountered when he returned to Kifoukourou was that of the Mata Sonapanga.

Sitting on a stool of cubic form, draped in a red carpet of English manufacture, with his feet on a tiger grass mat, the great chief of the Ormas was, as usual, flanked by his general staff of magicians. In addition, Most Serene Highnesses, foreigners of distinction, were forming a thick black semicircle around his seat of honor.

"Mousoungou," said the Sonapanga, in a dry tone, "look at the sky. The sun is already setting in the Tanganyika; the moon is rising. Is the banza Kisimbasimba in your power? Has the governor of the province asked you for *aman*? Has he sent, to make his surrender, a simple district chief? Has the governor of the besieged fort thought of sending you a negotiator? No, Kisimbasimba is not taken."

"That's true," Isidore replied. "The day is ended, and I haven't received any capitulatory visit. What do you want?"

"I'm your master."

"Which is to say that I've become your slave again. That's fair; I've lost the game. I made superb plans—but I had no luck at all."

"*Eyah!* I thought you were Ouaka's envoy; I thought you were a prophet. You're nothing but an impostor, a bad ganga-ya-ita."

"Your...."

"You shall die."

"Indeed. That's your right. I don't protest."

"You shall die, and when your soul has been taken back by Ouaka, perhaps we shall be delivered from the evil spirits that are denying us access to Kisimbasimba."

"So you believe that the city is inhabited by spirits? Well, let me tell you that's a load of rubbish?"

"I shall offer you as a sacrifice to Loubari, Mgoussa and Moussamouira."

"So be it. You see, I'd rather get it over with right way than listen to you talking such nonsense."

"You shall, moreover, have a fine funeral."

"Oh, that's all the same to me—except that I have one request to make before I smoke my last cigarette. I have two poor wretches with me: my black Arab and my mulatto. You know—the big baby who tells his beads to Mohammed and the lanky penguin who is always complaining that he's starving. One can't refuse anything to a man condemned to death, isn't that right? Well, let them alone and set them free, if that's within the scope of your bounty."

"Impossible."

"I'm asking you for a little pity for brave men who haven't done anything—or rather, they've only done what I've told them to do. If the city isn't taken, it's not their fault, it's mine."

"They'll follow you to Ouaka. Your Arab has committed sacrilege; he raised his hand to the sacred goats."

"What, you believe that! You, a young man from a good family! But the mulatto, at least, hasn't done any harm to anyone!"

"Death to that *soko!*"

"Chocolat! What have you got against him?"

73

"That soko, that gorilla, has unleashed the rage of the spirits against us, especially that of Mousammouira, who reigns over this place. His crime is that of having the evil eye."

"Don't you believe it! My poor Chocolat only has eyes for soup—but he has good ones, of course, indefatigable for good nourishment."

"All three of you shall die!"

"That's not new. You're going to put on a second performance of the other day's play. As you like! But quickly, if you please—tie us to the tree and shoot us right away."

"No, not this evening, and not shot under the tree. Tomorrow morning, when the sun reappears in the sky, you will be taken to the edge of the lake, to the summit of the rock of the soft grass; the Arab will be hoisted onto the round rock; the mulatto on top the rock in the form of a dog's head."

"Each to his Calvary, then."

"Then, at the same moment, at a signal from the chief of the magicians, you will be thrown into the lake."

"Well, that's not new. It recalls the famous rock near the Capitol of Toulouse."

A *coup de théâtre* cut short Isidore's ludicrous reflections. A hand fell on his shoulder; his torture commenced. He saw re-entering the stage the Kilombe, the Tringote and the Troumbachaganga, combining the effects of their lugubrious grimaces in chorus. The three torturers were accompanied by their usual valets.

Mimoun and Chocolat were apprehended, like their chief. The Tringlote, attaching herself to Mimoun as if to a prey lost and found again, showed the unfortunate spahi her long teeth, blackened by betel.

But what extraordinary torture is in preparation for the condemned men? By the light of the conflagration, which is not yet extinct, Isidore sees three large sacks brought forth, longer than those employed in his regiment to go for bread under the guidance of the company quartermaster and the orders of the duty captain.

What does that signify? The sacks are made of antelope skin. What are they going to do with that strange fabric?

The poor cook soon has the key to the mystery. Two of the executioner's valets hold the unfortunate Chocolat upright while a third puts a sack over his head, which comes down all the way to his feet. The mulatto is imprisoned like an umbrella in its sheath. He can be heard imploring his patron, San José de Cacuaco, who appears to have blocked his ears. The valets make the prisoner turn ninety degrees and lay him on the ground. Then the chief of the omen readers advances at a solemn pace and throws into the sack a yellow bird, a snake and a fish. That done, the aides seal the sack with the aid of a thick rope, which, measuring no less than two meters in length, is able to make twenty turns. The knot is solid.

The sack enclosed Chocolat is rolled into a corner; the jack-jack agitates madly, uttering moans and invoking San José incessantly, who remains deaf to his *in manos*.

It is Mimoun's turn. The procedure is the same, with the one aggravating difference that as the antelope skin shroud is about to be passed over him, the inexorable Tringlote comes to show him her grinding jaw one last time.

"Alhamulillah!"—Praise God—the impassive Muslim limits himself to saying, allowing himself to be incarcerated without putting up the slightest resistance.

The chief of the augurs puts into the sack a bird known as an *adjutant*, a small monkey and a lizard. It is secured and bound, and the stout cylinder is rolled alongside Chocolat's. Mimoun maintains a very dignified silence and immobility.

My turn now! Isidore says to himself. *My sack! To think that it will fit me like a glove! No, for sure, a ceremony like this isn't as interesting as one might think. It even lacks entertainment, considerably.*

With that, the poor ganga-ya-ita was subjected to the operation of being put in the sack. While he was being dressed, his thoughts took on a melancholy tint, the outcome of bitter consolations dictated to him by an invincible self-esteem.

This, he said to himself, *is what it is to be a true general. I'm meeting the fate of all great men. Look at Lafayette, that respectable old man, with his white horse and his white hair, and William Tell, and Belisarius, who was reduced to begging for alms with his helmet at the door of the Madeleine, and me, who is going to perish with his sack on his back!*

Isidore is soon clad in the antelope skin. The chief omen reader has given him for intimate companions a small rodent, a green bird and a lake fish. Then the worthy zouave is tied up and rolled side by side with his comrades.

With these preparations terminated, the Mata Sonapanga, his courtiers and his magicians have nothing more to do than wait patiently for dawn. Already, however, the spirits are manifestly placated, by virtue of the victims having been put in sacks. There is a downpour, which puts out the fires in the plain and preserves from imminent ruin all the bomas of the investment line.

To celebrate this first success, the Mata of the Ormas assembles his faithful followers in the hut nearest the point where the three sacks have been placed. He has enormous earthenware jars brought under the maize thatch, vats that are filled with pommbé. Slaves distribute bowls of woven straw to the great chief's guests, with long aspiration tubes in the form of gigantic bassoons. The entire company drinks; the sorghum beer is pumped in waves, while the rain falls in torrents outside.

In the meantime and *inter pocula*, the merry drinkers hold a kind of council of war. Yes, whatever it costs, they will take the insolent Kisimbasimba. Yes, the death of the victims will appease the anger of the spirits. In any case, they have seven army corps, each seventy thousand men strong, and if those troops are insufficient, they will summon others. They will call the entire Orma nation to the flag. In any case, the city will be taken; they swear it by Ouaka.

And they continue drinking the pommbé.

Enclosed in his sack, Isidore can hear what the drinkers are saying distinctly. When will they finish drinking and shouting? Personally, what he would like is a little peace and quiet, the time to collect himself before passing from life to death.

The former soldier has courage, but what is making him feel bad is Chocolat's persistent wailing. The unfortunate mulatto never ceases to moan, and to recite baroque prayers. Soon, there are horrible vociferations. He is doubtless dying of hunger, the poor fellow! Finally, his voice chokes; Isidore can no longer hear anything. The lanky fellow has doubtless forgotten the taste of bread, which he loved so much, permanently.

As for him, a ganga-ya-ita fallen from his splendors, if he has not yet rendered up his soul, he is not much better off. He can hardly breathe in his narrow prison. Asphyxia is imminent; it is not far off, because the rain that is falling in torrents is causing the antelope skin to shrink. But that is nothing compared to suffering thus from an absolute lack of air. Compressed within the walls of the enveloping sheath, the poor cook feels a sharp pain in the region of his heart. What's that? Oh, it's doubtless the snake beginning to bite. A mortal sting!

Well, so much the better, says Isidore to himself. *Better to finish it right away. Let the snake bleed me like a pullet, I don't care, in order not to die of choking like a fashionable ox.*

But the pain becomes intolerable. After long efforts, the prisoner succeeds in recovering a little liberty in one arm. He bends it, and succeeded in raising his hand to his heart, where the hideous reptile is sucking his blood.

No, it's not a snake attacked to its prey. What is it, then? Isidore's fingers have encountered something un-expected. That's what has stung him—yes, that's really what has wounded him! It's a foreign body, a small hard object, pointed like a nail. He recognizes it now. It's the tip of the long cavalry saber that he was carrying the day before, which burst into fragments when he was using it against the buffaloes whose tightly-knit ranks were ob-structing the breach of Kisimbasimba. How does that tip come to be pricking his chest?

Undoubtedly, at the moment when the blade splin-tered, that fragment of the broken weapon must have flown into his garments and stuck there, flat; then, when he was put in the sack, laid on the ground and rolled over, the piece of metal was displaced in such a way as to go into action. At any rate, it's necessary to remove it from the position it's occupying in front of his heart.

Isidore detaches the sharp point. It's no less than three centimeters long; easily equivalent to a serpent's tooth!

That's an idea, Isidore says to himself. *It's a tool, that little piece of sword blade. What if I were to try to make use of it? Why not? Let's have a go.*

The cook, so expert in preparing pieces of meat, succeeds—not without effort—in splitting the antelope skin. He makes an incision, a small solution of continuity. Finally, air gets in; he can breathe.

That success encourages him to continue. He goes to work; the skin is cut; the sack splits; the cylinder opens along a "ladder." The hole is soon large enough for an honest man to pass through. Like the old fool in *Les Fourberies de Scapin*,[20] Isidore eases himself out of the prison in the depths of which the three animals, his companions, have had the intelligence to remain quiet.

Now he is on his feet; he cocks an anxious ear to see whether anyone is coming. All is silence is the Kifoukourou camp, save for the monotonous sound of the rain. All the fires are extinct. As for the Mata Sonapanga, he is no longer drinking pommbé, having drunk enough of it to pass out. His courtiers are all around him, lying on the floor of the hut, dead dunk.

Another idea, the cook says to himself. *The Mata's asleep—what if I were to go? It's perfectly permissible to go since there's no longer anyone around and I have no need to ask for the latch to be lifted. Consequently, then...oh yes, wait a minute! I can't abandon the comrades like that. My brave Mimoun! My poor Chocolat!*

---

[20] The 1671 play by Molière—Scapin is the deceitful valet who continually puts one over on his master Léandre, the "old fool" to whom Isidore is referring.

Two imbeciles that don't know their ABCs, but good lads. I'll unstitch them.

Isidore advanced to set his companions free, and then had a great surprise. Mimoun's sack had disappeared! Chocolat's had a big hole in it. The mulatto had quit the antelope skin like a chick emerging from its egg!

Chapter IX
Kisimbasimba

Isidore could not, in all conscience, go in search of his two companions. He would have liked to save them, to enable them to share in his good fortune as they had shared the bad, but it would have been compromising his own safety, and his chances of salvation, to start searching the Kifoukourou lines trying to find them.

What had become of the aide-de-camp and the worthy chief of staff? The ganga-ya-ita had no idea. They were certainly no longer there, beside their chief. Poor Mimoun! Unfortunate Chocolat! They had doubtless been taken away, one to the round rock, the other to the summit of the dog's head. What was extraordinary, however, was that Chocolat's antelope skin was still there, in the ground. Had he been taken out of his sack, then, in order to climb his Calvary on foot? The circumstance was strange, to say the least.

Isidore did not have time to plumb the depths of the mystery. Without further reflection, but not without paying some tribute of regret to the two comrades who had vanished like shadows, he hastened to make himself scarce, without making any noise.

The camps were silent; all the Ormas seemed to be profoundly asleep, as is the prerogative of brave men whose consciences are clear. The fugitive had quickly got out of the boma. Nevertheless, he was fearful of the advance posts.

One sentinel, who happened to be awake, attempted, albeit timidly, to bar his way. Fortunately, the cook was still wearing the brilliant uniform of a ganga-ya-ita; the sentinel, knowing his métier, did not fail to present arms to him, in conformity with the prescriptions of national regulations regarding the service of armies of campaign—which is to say that he threw himself to the ground, face down.

Finally, Isidore is outside the lines. He is saved! The surrounding area is deserted; everything there is calm; no sound can any longer be heard, save for the distant snuffling of hippopotamuses and the bellowing of bullfrogs. En route!

The fugitive starts running, but at the first stride his foot skids on the damp earth. He falls over, hands and face forward, but without doing himself any harm, for he has only projected himself into mud.

He gets up and sets off again. As if to console him for that fall and give him courage, the rain stops. In the east, the first light is making the clouds iridescent.

Oh, how beautiful the dawn is on a day of deliverance! The master cook can no longer contain himself when he hears the sound of birdsong. Perhaps it's the one that he had on his head a little while ago inside his antelope skin. Evidently, it's cheerful. It's a beautiful day!

Decidedly, thinks the happy runaway, *it's all going well*.

He has just burst into laughter when he perceives that he has two black hands, like those of a negro. He understands why. His fall a little while ago took place at one of the sites of the previous day's conflagration. The carbonized substances, mixed by the torrents of rain, have produced a mud resembling greasepaint. He concludes that his face must have the same color as his hands, but, given the situation he is in, such a disguise is not to be disdained.

And he starts laughing again, thinking about the Sonapanga.

It's at the present moment, he thinks, *that the great Mata of the devil's army was proposing to offer me to his Mgoussa and the other Loubaris, and all the fine spirits of Lake Tanganyika. Hurrah for liberty!*

What is he going to do with his reconquered liberty, however? Or rather—a burning question—is it really liberty? Having escaped, against all hope, from his animal skin sheath, the joyful cook has done little more than change prisons. He is still surrounded by a circle of iron. Instead of orientating himself in such a way as to reach open country, he has fled without thinking about it in the direction of Kisimbasimba. The investment lines are enveloping him; the field in which he is able to move freely only extends within the zone between those lines and the fortifications of the besieged stronghold. It is impossible to find any place of refuge whatsoever in that terrain of assaults; he will soon be discovered there. It is impossible to get out, because it would be necessary to pierce the lines. In any case, what lies beyond that obstacle is difficult to overcome. The land of servitude, of slavery. He would be quickly collected there.

In that situation, without any apparent exit, Isidore makes a heroic decision, as befits a zouave. He tells himself that there is, for the present, only one thing to do: to hurl himself into Kisimbasimba, to enter into the service of its defenders, to place himself at the disposal of the people he was fighting yesterday.

Not sparing the compliments, he thought that the idea was eminently luminous, that the solution was all the more practical because he could not see any other, that that light of hope was the only one shining on the horizon. He repeated to himself that he was not taking any risk, that he had nothing to lose in attempting this last chance; that the defenders would no doubt be glad to give him shelter; that, if they refused or took it into their heads to kill him, that death would, after all, be neither better nor worse than any other; that one only ever dies once, and that, all things considered, it was better to finish with an intolerable life.

Having thus ripened his resolution, the former soldier headed swiftly toward the place, not without audaciously comparing his fate to that of Napoléon going, on the advice of someone called Themistocles, to sit down "in the shadow of the British hearth."

In no time at all he was at the foot of the palisade that had been breached the day before. A further surprise! That breach, so broadly opened, had been blocked. The defense had taken care to plant more palings of hard wood in place of those that the assailants had torn up.

From which it appears, thought Isidore, *that the city isn't deserted, as the Sonapanga claims.*

Conveniently remembering the lessons in gymnastics that had been given to him in the regiment, he succeeded in getting over the latticework barrier, took the familiar route, and reached the foot of the palisade, which he had breached by means of fire, in a few strides. That opening had been blocked, too. A mysterious hand, operating from the inside, had caused any solution of continuity to vanish by lining up numerous jointed tree trunks throughout the width of the passage. The banza was obviously not abandoned.

The former zouave, agile and brisk, jammed his fingertips into the joints in the wall, and the tips of his toes in fissures in the wood, and climbed in that fashion to the crest of the little rampart, swiftly passed his legs over it and jumped down on the other side.

There, other difficulties were about to materialize.

The majority of Europeans doubtless have no suspicion that there are relatively considerable banzas, or fortresses, in the heart of Africa. That is, however, a fact whose reality has been duly attested by voyagers.

Sir Samuel Baker speaks of large fortified places, destroyed today, the sites of which can only be recognized by the sacred fig tree that sheltered the forum and the tall euphorbias that formed its perimeter.[21]

Stanley mentions at the foot of the mountains of Ourougourou the city of Simbamouenni, founded in the territory of the Ouakami by the famous Kisabengo, the leader of maroon slaves turned bandit; Ougounda, thrice besieged, but in vain, by another brigand by the name of Mirambo; Ouilianjouorou, blockaded by Arab traffickers; and Kirira, taken by storm by Seid ben Hamid.

Cameron cites, in the course of his account of his voyages, the fortresses of Kaouela, Kammbala and a number of other centers of population carefully put in a state of defense.[22]

In all those banzas, the voyagers expressly distinguished components similar to those of our European fortifications; they make mention of continuous enclo-

---

[21] Samuel White Baker, the discovery of Albert-Nyanza (Lake Albert) had set out to discover the source of the Nile; his first memoir of his expedition was *The Albert N'yanza, Great Basin of the Nile* (1866). He subsequently ventured into popular fiction in *Cast Up by the Sea* (1868).

[22] Verney Lovett Cameron, the first European to cross Africa from the shore of the Indian Ocean to the Atlantic shore, published *Across Africa* in 1877.

sures with escarpment, ditch and counterescarpment, battlements, embrasures, etc. As for the size of these fortified locations, one can appreciate them in accordance with Mr. Stanley's assertion, which attributed a thousand houses and five thousand inhabitants to the site of Simbaouenni.

That of Kisimbasimba appeared even more remarkable by virtue of the great accumulation of complicated defenses. Beyond the wooden stockade, facing it, rose up a stone wall more than three meters high.

With a vigorous leap, Isidore jumped up to grab hold of the coping stone, which he seized with both hands, pulled himself up to support himself on his elbows, and then succeeded in sitting on top of the wall. There he scanned the horizon.

No one! He could not perceive anyone. Was there truly not a soul inside this marvelous fortress? But in that case, who had repaired the palisade and the stockade? The breaches had certainly not closed by themselves!

Intrigued, Isidore let himself slide down the wall. Then he saw a hedge of mimosas blocking his passage— a hedge preceded by a wide ditch full of water. The fugitive had expended a lot of effort since his escape, and, given that the sun was already shining ardently, he was tormented by thirst. He went to the ditch in order to draw water from it and refresh himself—but when he reached the edge, he recoiled....

In spite of being thoroughly accustomed to extraordinary things, a frisson had run through him.

That was because the green waters of the ditch, which was twenty meters broad, were swarming with an entire population of monsters: crocodiles, monitors, freshwater sharks, electric eels and large water snakes; a vast throng of beasts analogous to the ichthyosaurs and megalosaurs that one sees in atlases appended to treatises on paleontology; an interlacement of reptiles, a museum of viscous hydras and hideous dragons!

How could a gulf so horribly inhabited by crossed? The unfortunate cook, dying of thirst, wandered along the bank of that Tenarus for a long time.[23] Finally, he succeeded in finding a means of passage, albeit a scabrous means.

But when one does not have the luxury of making a choice, he said to himself, with justice, *it's necessary to use the only thing one has at one's disposal.*

That unique means of communication consisted of a stone dam that cut across the ditch at right angles to the two banks. The crest was as trenchant at the summit of a steeply pitched roof, but Isidore did not hesitate. He sat astride it bravely. Making a mobile support of his hands, he made his crossing "on horseback" on the ridge, straddling it, not without shivering a little under the gleam of so many pupils with milky tints and so many green gazes aimed at him.

He remembered, as he "rode" in that fashion, the stirring legend those Portuguese-Congolese sailors like to relate, of the Allibamba. It is the story of a file of nine chained slaves that were swallowed in one go by a ferocious caiman. The saurian could not digest the iron chain that bound them together. It died, and the shipboard surgeon who autopsied it found all the links of the chain in its stomach. Those chains, of strong iron, were admira-

---

[23] The reference is to the river Tenarus, where Alaric the Goth allegedly had to put new heart into his troops on the way to sack Rome.

bly scoured and corroded by gastric juices. A little while longer, and the caiman would have digested the metal.

Isidore—who, in his capacity as a Provençal, always liked to have the last word—had then replied that in his native land, in the bay of Toulon and even in Marseilles, the crocodiles had no difficulty swallowing harmoniflutes and bicycle wheels, not to mention naval howitzers, all of which they digested very well…which was proven by the fact that no traces of them was ever found in their entrails.

At that critical moment, Isidore was not laughing. He was observing and struggling against vertigo. Finally, he came ashore safe and sound on the opposite bank, got through the hedge—not without snagging his clothes and cutting his face on it.

When he emerged on the other side he thought he was inside the city.

Wrong!

Before his eyes a cyclopean wall loomed up, in carved stone masonry, after the fashion of certain Tuscan palazzos In front of that sheer face opened yet another ditch. This one, excavated in the rock, was divided by sets of wooden stakes into a number of distinct compartments, presenting the appearance of one of the menageries that one encounters in the courts of petty African kings, of which Speke has give us a gripping description.[24] It was a series of leopard boxes, panther cages, kennels of huge dogs, ditches of savage wolves and rhinoceros lodges. There were other beasts there, too, which it was impossible to see. Wild boars could be

---

[24] John Hanning Speke published *Journal of the Discovery of the Source of the Nile* in 1863.

heard grunting, felines roaring, buffaloes bellowing and elephants trumpeting.

A subtle sense of smell revealed to the carnivores the unexpected presence of a human being. Then a frightful concert of strangled roars, muted bellowings, grim moans and prolonged growls rose up.

Only the great dogs, their hackles rising, did not bark. They were standing still, on guard.

Good, Isidore said to himself. *Better and better. And that Mata thinks the city is only haunted by spirits! Those spirits are beasts, then? They've been changed into nurses, like Nabuchodonosor, the gallant knight of the Sleeping Beauty. What a zoo!*

With that, taking his courage in both hands once again, the valiant zouave passed "on horseback" over the crest of one of the wooden partitions and arrived without a hitch at the foot of the solid escarpment. It was an enormous wall, decorated at the base by colossal statues carved out of the granite. The place where he had arrived was ornamented by figures of elephants, caryatids of grandiose proportions, serving as supports for a megalithic monument.

He was casting a surprised glance over the stone elephants when he perceived, at the base of a pilaster, a stone thimble hollowed out by time, the hollow of which the rain had filled with water, already troubled by dust. He was bending down in order to drink in the manner of Gideon's soldiers when he perceived an elephant that seemed an image of death itself....

But the beast really was alive; it resembled Moonchild, the good Matoto, but its eye had a mocking gaze.

Isidore thought that he was doomed. He wanted to flee, but where, and how?

The elephant, wrapping its trunk around him gently, pushed him in a certain direction.

After walking for a few moments, the beast stopped the traveler at a place where the masonry of the sheer wall disappeared, masked by a pile of tree trunks superimposed horizontally between two rows of vertical stakes.

As if with a skillful hand, the trunk delicately lifted up those wooden logs one by one, and exposed the narrow entrance to a grotto whose ceiling was barely as high as a man's height. At ground level there was a rippling spring whose water ran toward the far wall.

Then the pachyderm started shifting its weight from one foot to another in an amiable fashion, as if to invite its guest to refresh himself. Isidore, who was dying of thirst, welcomed the invitation.

When he had finished drinking, he turned his head toward the entrance of the cavern.

The entrance had just been closed; the elephant had replaced all the pieces of wood, without any joints.

The grotto was hermetically sealed.

Chapter X
The Spirits and the Beasts

"Good," said Isidore, aloud. "Well played! My compliments, Monsieur Elephant. Whoever trained you was clever, and you know your métier. You truly put humans in the shade. As for me, it was written that I'd only get out of one prison to pass into another. At least I've had a drink…I was thirsty. What if I were to try to get some sleep now, while awaiting…what? I don't know what, for, in truth, I can expect anything."

However, Isidore could not dissimulate his surprise when, searching for a place to lie down in the depths of the grotto, he was abruptly dazzled by a beam of light that illuminated the walls. A little doorway had just opened at the back, which had been drowned in shadows a moment before; it was just broad enough and high enough to give passage to a man.

The prisoner did not hesitate to go through it.

A new surprise! The elephant was standing on the other side of the threshold, still shifting its weight from one stout leg to another.

Isidore understood that the grotto of the spring fulfilled the function of a postern in the fortifications of Kisimbasimba; that he had just come though a passageway opened in the thickness of the rampart; and that the friendly elephant was nothing but a door keeper posted to guard the passage. But what route had the exceedingly well-trained elephant taken itself, in order to open the secret door of the cavern, as it had just done? Why was it granting him, an Orma deserter, the honor of a private entry? Following what instinct, or what instructions, was it inviting him to penetrate into this place? That was what it was difficult to comprehend.

Once through the wicket gate, Isidore thought that he would be in the city—but no; he emerged on to a broad esplanade, and the said esplanade was strewn with small obstacles known in military terminology as "accessory defenses." Here, the ground was littered with a myriad of shells, bristling with spurs—shells of the genus *Murex*, which, no matter how one drops them on the ground, always fall with one spur upwards; there, a forest of wooden spikes of unequal height sprang up, planted irregularly, but all with sharp points hardened by fire; elsewhere, other, stronger spikes emerged from the round, arranged in quincunxes; there were attached pikes, through at the neck of which narrow thongs of hippopotamus hide were passed, thongs extended in bizarre interlacements in such a way as to constitute inextricable networks; further away opened conical holes and profound ditches, at the bottom of which leopards with ardent eyes were prowling.

The elephant that was guiding Isidore indicated a pathway across that difficult terrain that was free of any obstacle. Preceding him along, it led him to a wall that closed the esplanade to the north. It was a strange closure, because it was bristling over its entire surface with long spikes that forbade anyone to approach, in the manner of the pieces of broken glass that garnish the coping stones of our walls. There was no broken glass there, though: each hedgehog spine was nothing but an elephant tusk or a rhinoceros horn. The wall offered the aspect of a long plank of ivory nails.

The elephant pointed out a small door set in the base of that unapproachable bank, armored with hippopotamus hide. Its trunk cleverly released the catch; then, having passed its man through the narrow opening, it closed the door behind him.

This time, Isidore really was in the city.

His gaze embraced the view.

An admirable site! From the ivory wall to the shores of the Tanganyika, Kisimbsimba was staged like an amphitheater. The diameter of that hemicycle, which measured no less than a kilometer from north to south, melted away in soft hues into the mists of the shore. From the point where he was standing, the visitor could see the blue expanse of the lake—an expanse bordered on the horizon by a fringe of mountain chains in red and prismatic tones. He could see the waves of the Caspian known as Tanganyika—meaning "collector of the waters"—breaking at the foot of the banza.

The center of the amphitheater was indented sharply to design a little harbor, which terminated in a bottleneck on the side of the water. Inside that cove, encased by steep high rocks, fell a foaming sheet of water, a cascade similar to that of the Fontaine de Vaucluse. That was the mouth of a river whose upper reaches escaped the gaze. Before pouring this into the harbor of Kisimbasimba, the river probably passed beneath the city in a tunnel. Its tumultuous waters were endowed with a monumental outflow, the natural architecture of which was reminiscent to that of the door of a fort—or, better still, the porch of a Gothic church. Under that porch, flocks of large birds seemed brilliant dots set against a black background.

As for the city, its appearance was extraordinary, for it offered nothing to the eye but a mosaic of large edifices, islets or groups of huts in the form of beehives, ruins invaded by brushwood, debris corroded by grass, oases of palm trees, groves of sycamores and clumps of mimosas: silence and solitude everywhere; an immense city, but a dead city, crumbling under the hammer of the centuries!

Isidore advanced through those desolate terrains, astonished to encounter there pyramids, arches and colonnades. Such architecture in the very heart of Africa was, he told himself, implausible! He admired here the arches of a cistern analogous to the one that Cameron identified in Ouvinnza; there the remains of a temple similar to that of Isamboul in Nubia; further on, the entrance to a hypogeum lined with colossal statues; everywhere, the stumps of columns, capitals and blocks of stone were heaped up pell-mell, dislocated or broken.

What struck the cook most of all was the profusion of sculptures spread over the walls of the monuments of the mysterious city, as silent and deserted as an ancient necropolis. On the rock of the hypogeum he saw a group similar to the one that Cameron noticed in a village of the Onnyanyembe: a group formed by a seated man with, at his sides, a wild goat, a large African dog, and a tom-tom or gongong.

He admired the figures of humans and animals that decorated the facades of cisterns, palaces or temples. In all the bas-reliefs, uniformly representing hunting scenes or episodes of war, he observed that the dominant figure was that of the lion. In all the pictures that flashed before his eyes, the lion, the symbol of courage and strength, seemed to be domesticated by humans, to be obeying him as a master, accompanying him hunting, assisting him in battles, lending him at every opportunity the aid of its claws.

Was that the origin of the name Kisimbasimba, the city of lions, as the Ormas called it? Did that name reproduce, like a faithful echo, that of a favorite emblem of ancient art?

Isidore was wondering that when, moving through the ruins, he arrived at the edge of a vast ditch.

At the bottom of that ditch there were lions! No longer symbolic lions, or lions playing a role in human history, carved in marble or sculpted in granite, but real lions of flesh and bone, very much alive, uttering respectable roars.

A hundred meters from that one, there was another similar ditch, similarly inhabited; then, a hundred meters further on, another ditch...and then another!

Those cavities, conical in form, were methodically arranged like *trous-de-loup* in front of the earthworks of a campaign—except that, instead of a wolf, there were thirty big cats in each of the ditches.

Decidedly, Kisimbasimba really was the city of lions.

Evidently, it was from these numerous ditches that the defenders had taken their lions with the bloody tails, the heroes of the day before who had mauled the assailants so badly!

But where in this astonishing city were those invisible defenders? What were they? Spirits or beasts?

As for humans, the cook said to himself, *as for humans...but that isn't possible. And yet, in truth, there are beasts that have so much intelligence, and intelligent humans who are so bestial! Oh, in truth, I'm losing my mind, I'll throw my tongue to the cats....*

Suspicion—a dolorous suspicion—invaded Isidore's mind, battering a breach in his shaky reason. The former drummer in the zouaves, who had mocked the Sonapanga so blithely for his robust faith in the Spirits of the Lake, was wondering whether the Orma gangas might not have plausible reasons for believing in Loubari and Mgoussa, and even the hobgoblin Mousammouira.

He was beginning to stray into the most absurd hypotheses when he was suddenly seized by several pairs of vigorous hands.

An opaque black veil was placed over his head, his hands and feet were bound, and he was wrapped up in his large ganga-ya-ita's cloak in less than a minute.

He was lifted up then, like an Egyptian mummy, and, having been briskly loaded onto robust shoulders, felt himself being borne away, so to speak, by an express train.

His abductors ran like Muslims carrying a corpse to a cemetery.

Chapter XI
Preludes to a Great Expedition

So, Isidore said to himself, philosophically, *it appears that it's not over! Quite frankly, though, for mere spirits, their grip is a bit strong. I was wondering whether they were spirits or beasts—well, they're human! I was quite certain, myself, that there was someone in this establishment, that the city wasn't defending itself all by itself! Who are these people? Brigands, probably, like those I've just quit...similar, at any rate! Perhaps they're going to propose to me that I defend their fortifications, and pass me off as the governor elect of the place...which would be amusing. But how they can run! Where the devil are they taking me? What the devil's got into them?*

After a frantic steeplechase of rather long duration, Isidore felt himself deposited—or, rather, dropped, on the ground.

Finally, he thought, *the spectacle is about to begin. I'm going to find out whom I'm dealing with.*

In fact, obliging hands, albeit a trifle rough, removed the thick veil that covered his head. He could see clearly!

He saw....

"Why," he cried, "it's Samanou! And there's Popo! And all the Biribis! What the devil are you up to here, you old jokers?"

The five or six fellows making up the band were momentarily stunned. They seemed to have recognized Isidore's voice. They wanted to believe their ears—but

97

not their eyes, however, for the human being who was speaking to them was wearing the costume of the general officers of the enemy army, and had a face and hands as black as a negro's.

Then one of the abductors—the one that the prisoner had called Samanou—experienced a flash of enlightenment. He picked up a cloth soaked in water and wiped the mud off Isidore's face. The mat complexion of the French cook appeared in its natural state.

Immediately, exclamations burst forth.

"Mossi Tizidour! Mossi Tizidour!" brayed the people who had just kidnapped the former ganga-ya-ita, in chorus.

And, while making a fuss of him, they freed their captive from the aloe ropes that bound his arms and legs. Then they took him affectionately under the arms, drew him along for a few paces, leading him to the threshold of a hut in front of which stood a flagpole. At the top of the pole floated the French colors.

Isidore understood.

That reed hut was nothing other than the general quarters of the mission from which events had so violently separated him. He was about to recover his masters!

Well, he said to himself, not without emotion, *that's something else I didn't expect!*

"Mossi Tizidour!" the chorus resumed. "Mossi Tizidour!"

At those cries of furious joy, several people came out of the hut. They were Europeans.

Isidore, who recognized them, hurled himself toward them. "Oh!" he cried, in a tearful voice. "Oh, Commandant, it's you! You, Monsieur Duvivier! And you, Monsieur Cornelius! Is it possible that I've found you again? Is that really you, Major? And you, Monsieur Chaplain!"

It was too much for his long-overexcited nerves. The ex-commanding general could no longer contain himself. He was weeping copiously; emotion was choking him, and he was heard to sob.

But that was only momentary. He told his story, briefly, and when he was asked for news of his two companions in misfortune, he replied with a certain ill-humor: "I'm very much afraid that Mimoun is, at the present moment, in Mohammed's paradise, and as for Chocolat, I suspect he's been cooked!"

The Europeans that Isidore had just recognized did, indeed, comprise the general staff of the mission to which he had attached himself in the capacity of cook.

The man that he had addressed as Commandant appeared to be about thirty-seven or thirty-eight years of age; he was a man of medium height and robust constitution, with intelligent eyes and features imprinted with energy. His name was Beautemps-Fresnel, and he held the rank of frigate-captain in the French navy.

Monsieur Duvivier, the expedition's engineer, seemed to be about the same age. Afflicted with premature baldness and a trifle corpulent, he had large prominent eyes shielded by enormous spectacles. Almost the same height as Monsieur Thiers,[25] his physiognomy radiated the same vivacity, the same sagacity and the same devouring activity as that of the illustrious statesman.

The savant Professor Cornelius formed a contrast with the engineer, for he was tall, elegantly dressed and, although he had probably doubled the cape of fifty, was

---

[25] The French statesman Adolphe Thiers was notoriously short—even shorter than Napoléon—at five foot one.

absolutely scornful of the threat of obesity. He had a handsome face with placid features, one of these serene visages that characterize the adepts of elevated philosophical science, which one cannot forget, once seen.

The person that Isidore had addressed as "Major" was named Cyprien Quentin. He was a young military doctor, whose smiling face announced an uncommon vigor. Like Monsieur Cornelius, he was tall but thin, and temperamentally severe—very apt, in consequence, to support privations and fatigues.

Finally, the chaplain attached to the staff of the mission was the Abbé de Couédic. He was an old Breton priest, as straight as an Italian poplar, whose body was endowed with a solidity proof against anything, with a head like Saint Jerome's, a physiognomy permeated with mildness, courage and faith.

Those five men, who were standing side by side on the threshold of an intertropical African *gourbi*, were almost in uniform. They were wearing gray woolen garments, trousers and jackets, with broad belts, also woolen, around their waists; their legs protruded from long leather gaiters. Coiffed with cork helmets, proof against the acuity of the solar rays, they were holding rifles that seemed to have become their inseparable companions.

How had those five voyagers, cast by fortune into a deserted banza, found themselves abandoned there in the last days of March 1877? How had their enterprise begun, and how had it been, to all appearances, diverted from its path?

The original idea for a voyage of exploration in the African continent had been Monsieur Duvivier's. A collaborator of Gustave Lambert, he had dreamed for a long time of departing with his friend for the North Pole, but poor Lambert had been killed on the day of Buzenval. Suddenly, all the plans for the expedition had collapsed without leaving anyone a glimpse of a possible realization. That was what the engineer had ended up convincing himself, after a number of fruitless steps and three long years of vain expectation, between 1871 and 1874.

Then, having tested other possibilities in the wind, he had boldly turned his sail toward Africa. From the North Pole, which he had embraced for such a long time, his gaze made a hundred-and-eighty degree turn, directing itself toward the equator. What did the location of the goal to be attained matter, provided that, in the course of its pursuit, one had to expend intelligence, to furnish hard work, and to develop activity? Following that new program, the ardent Duvivier had begun by ensuring himself of the collaboration of three traveling companions.

One of them, Beautemps-Fresnel, had already taken part in one great scientific expedition, that of the exploration of the Mekong, directed by the unfortunate but illustrious Doudart de Lagrée.[26] He had been linked by friendship to another martyr of science, the intrepid Francis Garnier, killed under the walls of Hanoi, the capital of Tonkin, on 31 December 1873.

The second, Cornelius Bernard, who was known simply as Cornelius, in order not to be confused by virtue of homonymy with his illustrious friend Claude Bernard, had also undertaken great voyages. He owed his celebrity to the remarkable methods of which he had

---

[26] Ernest Doudart de Lagrée led the French Mekong Expedition of 1866-68, which he did not survive, leaving its completion to his second-in-command Francis Garnier, who was subsequently killed in action against insurrectionists.

been the first to make use in the course of an expedition to the Dead Sea, an exploration accomplished under the auspices of the Duc de Luynes.[27]

The third, Dr. Quentin, was also no novice, for he had visited the oasis of Ghadamès with Victor Largeau and had manifested, during the crossing of the Sahara, the qualities denoting a great voyager.[28]

"With the aid of these energetic men," Duvivier had said to himself, "it's impossible not to succeed."

"Beautemps-Fresnel will take on the military direction of the expedition; he's accustomed to command, understands men very well—civilized men as well as savages—and he's calm, patient and prudent. Everything will go well. He will also take charge of astronomical observations, in his capacity as a naval officer.

"Cornelius will study questions of anthropology and ethnography. An honorary member of the French Antiquarian Society, corresponding with all the geographical societies in the world, he's an eminent archeologist and philologist who can't fail to make precious discoveries with which the geographical sciences will be enriched.

"Young Quentin will make observations in meteorology, natural history, geology, zoology and botany.

For myself, I'll reserve the supervision of the equipment, construction work, topographical measure-

---

[27] Honoré Théodoric d'Albert, Duc de Luynes (1802-1867) assembled a vast collection of antiquities at the Château de Dampierre, and sponsored several expeditions, traveling himself to the Dead Sea and Petra in 1864.

[28] Victor Largeau—the father of the more famous Victor Emanuel Largeau, who played a major role in the creation and colonization of Chad—published two accounts of his attempts to cross the Sahara and reach Timbuktu in 1875 and 1877.

ments, making drawings and sketches, and writing the log."

It was in accordance with that program that the organization of the expedition had proceeded. The organization was easy, because they had at their disposal for that purpose a sum of five hundred thousand francs originating from a legacy from the late Admiral   . Thanks to the munificence of that excellent man, lost prematurely to science, the explorers had not had to worry about questions of money.

At the beginning of January 1875 Commandant Beautemps-Fresnel had charted the *Biafra* of Liverpool, one of the fastest ships of the Africa Steamship Company, which operated the service to Madeira, Tenerife and the West Coast of Africa, and had ordered the fitting out of the powerful vessel.

The baggage train designed to accompany the voyagers in the course of their expedition had been formed according to a judicious method that might stand as a model of its kind. The material objects, chosen with the greatest discernment, as many in France as in England, had been classified under distinct headings, such as clothing, camping equipment, subsistence, medicine, lighting, weapons, tools, instruments of observation, various apparatuses, money, trade goods, musical instruments, children's toys, etc. A few special crates enclosed a library of books of Africa bequeathed by the Admiral, stuffed with precious documents.

All this material, divided into a large number of parcels, each light enough not to exceed the load of two men, had been collected and stowed aboard the *Biafra*. The embarkation had been completed on 22 March.

Commandant Fresnel had, at the same time, proceeded with the recruitment of good personnel. In spite of his strict standards regarding age, health, temperament, character, knowledge and professional devotion, he had succeeded in recruiting nine former long-haul captains or naval officers, four naturalist-physicians and four missionary-chaplains.

He had also hired twenty-five artisan workers: carpenters, mechanics, smiths, weavers and agriculturalists. Finally, he had gone in quest of a cook. Having excellent reasons for obtaining a good one, he had, acting on precise information, made a sumptuous offer to Isidore, then sous-chef at the Grand Hotel. The echoes of that edifice had retained the memory of the dialogue that had taken place between the contracting parties.

"Your name is Isidore Chauvelot?"

"Present, Commandant. That's it. My father was named Chauvelot, my godfather Isidore, with the result that…"

"You've served in the zouaves?"

"I'm proud to have done so, Commandant, and pleased. Yes, I spent five years with the 1st jackals, third of the two. No punishments, clean record and a certificate—here it is…."

"I know that your conduct in the regiment was good; you're also a meritorious cook…."

"Meritorious! Oh, the Commandant is very kind. I'm only a scientist, for what is cooking, after all, but advanced chemistry? Only a scientist!"

"So be it. Would you like to enter my service?"

"Why not?"

"Because I'm undertaking a long voyage."

"I'm with you, Commandant."

"A longer voyage than you doubtless suppose; I'm leaving for Africa."

"Oh, as for Africa, it's a long time since I was there the first time. I can say that I know it well. I began my stint at Koleah. Then I was sent on detachment to Medeah, and then to Laghouat, and then…."

"It's not a matter of Algeria, but a region that neither you nor I know; I'm talking about equatorial Africa."

"Equa…oh, that's different, that must be in the south."

"A long way south of Medeah, and even of Laghouat. I owe you the whole truth. Many voyagers who have gone into that region haven't come back."

"The imbeciles!"

"The country that I'm proposing to explore is doubtless populated by anthropophages."

"Anthropo…?"

"People who eat human flesh, and might, in consequence, eat you."

"Eat me? Me, a cook! A man who enables others to eat! I'd like to see that!"

"That's not all. We'll have to brave wild beasts, live under a leaden sun—a sun whose ardent rays will subject us relentlessly to a frightful ambient temperature."

"Oh, of course, of course, if it's ambient, that's something else! But come on, Commandant, what do you expect me to do about it?"

"We'll have to endure fatigue, hunger and thirst."

"As long as we can smoke!"

"We'll suffer from fever; our lives will be incessantly exposed to perils of every sort."

"You're telling me so much, Commandant, that you'll end up making me believe that you think Isidore Chauvelot can be scared."

"I repeat that we'll be running countless dangers, and for two or three years."

"Two or three years! It's longer than going around the world, then?"

"You've been warned—think about it."

"It's done, Commandant; I'm your man."

"Good—sign this contract."

The Grand Hotel's cook had then placed at the bottom of the piece of paper that was held out to him a signature ornamented with the most improbable calligraphic flourishes, saying to himself complacently: *He's good one, the Commandant, if he thinks he can scare Isidore Chauvelot!*

Thus had been sealed the pact that linked Isidore to his master.

All the people called upon to take part in the expedition had been summoned to Paris for the 20 March; they all made the rendezvous. On 25 March, after receiving a telegram informing him that the fitting out was complete, Commandant Fresnel, having given his orders for departure, left for Liverpool himself with his domestic, Joseph, and his new cook, Isidore.

As they were about to leave Paris, the former sous-chef at the Grand Hotel, the savant chemist, had been somewhat surprised to hear Joseph asking the coachman to take them to the Gare du Nord.

"What! The Gare du Nord!" he had exclaimed. "But that doesn't make sense, since we're going south, into the ambient temperature!"

And when Joseph had sketched a smile, he had added, to himself: *Well, now there's a chap getting his four cardinal points mixed up. He doesn't even know his physics!*

The personnel of the expeditionary corps having been duly embarked, all the material objects being in order, the *Biafra* had made haste to put on steam, and, her pressure obtained, to quit her moorings. The departure from Liverpool had been affected in the evening of 30 March 1875, and a week later, the voyagers had made a port of call at Madeira.

During the journey, an amicable acquaintance had been struck up between Isidore and Professor Cornelius. The aura of an irresistible attraction drew toward one another those two men from two different worlds, in terms of their social condition, status and intelligence. By virtue of the force that sometimes resides in the law of contrasts, they proved sympathetic. Such a derogation of the usual pattern of life would have remained absolutely inexplicable to the other passengers if they had not divined that a contract of exchange had been agreed between the two parties.

In the manner of an illustrious painter whose unique pretention was being able to play the violin, the former sous-chef at the Grand Hotel, the doctor of sauces, had the mania of taking himself seriously, of listening to himself and admiring himself when, under the pretext of seeking to educate himself, he talked about science or literature. Now, the eminent professor of the Collège de France, the prince of the scientific world, lent an indulgent ear to the cook's blunders, corrected the most monstrous of his enormities in an affable tone and gently pruned his fantastic errors. More than that—he sometimes let them go.

From what source was the good professor—a man who often treated his best students and laureates of the Institute harshly—drawing these treasures of extreme indulgence? It is necessary to say, to his credit or his shame, that the excellent Cornelius had a chronic affliction. "One does not choose to be a gourmand," Brillat-Savarin said. Well, without wanting to be, the professor was a gourmand; he was infatuated with the delicacies so nicely concocted by Isidore's hand, and, out of respect for the indisputable talents of such a laboratory assistant, he let his fantasies pass, allowed him to chatter, pampered him like a favorite student whose tutor he was. With the result that between the contracting parties it had been tacitly stipulated that one would do the science, the other the cookery, and that, in those conditions, everything would be for the best. On witnessing the fact of that admirable concord, which was perhaps his work, Commandant Fresnel had carefully refrained from smiling.

From Madeira they had headed for Saint Louis in Senegal, where they had enrolled the spahi Mimoun-ben-Abdallah, whom destiny called one day to be the chief of the French cook's general staff.

From Saint Louis, the *Biafra* had descended to the equator, traveling along the coast.

In Monrovia, they had engaged the Krouman Biribis and the Ashanti Amonquatia; at Kibinda, all the chiefs of the secondary services had been taken on: Samanou, Dede, Popo, Ambacca, Punha, Kalkali and Congo.

After a long coastal navigation the *Biafra* had finally moored at Saint Paul de Loanda on 28 May 1875.

It was at Saint Paul that they had enrolled guides and *pagazis*—baggage porters—among whom was Chocolat, a hungry individual whose adventures were to make him famous. Isidore was proud of having invented him. Having heard him babbling in kitchen Latin, having seen him lifting enormous weights on the quay and then swallowing heaps of nourishment, the cook had said to Monsieur Fresnel:

"Commandant, without commanding you, I have a few words to say to you. You see that great imbecile over there? Well, he isn't as stupid as he looks. He takes responsibility, that one, for juggling with bales. And with regard to *mangearia*, I can vouch for his capacity. It's better than the old story of the cuirassiers of the guard. Hire me that fellow, and you won't be sorry."

And Chocolat had been enrolled in the list of the expedition's agents.

They had only remained at the dock at Saint Paul for the time strictly necessary for recruitment and renewal of food supplies, in addition to the official visits due to the Portuguese authorities. That done, they hastened to raise the anchor.

Having set a southward course once again, the *Biafra* had entered into the Kwanza, the river so well explored by Mr. Alexanderson of the Geographical Society of London.[29]

Going up the river, which was regularly traveled by a number of English vessels, the French expedition had arrived at Cambambe, a Portuguese outpost on the right bank 180 miles from the mouth. There the river navigation had ended, for it is above Cambambe that the Kwanza is blocked by the first cataract. Now, as Isidore said, who had heard mention of it at the Grand Hotel, "to operate on the cataract of a river would be the ultimate

---

[29] Carl Alexanderson, F.R.G.S. is virtually forgotten today, although his exploration of the Kwanza is mentioned in Verney Lovett Cameron's *Across Africa*, where the author undoubtedly discovered it.

challenge to an oculist's talent—and that kind of talent doesn't run around the streets."

In consequence, the *Biafra* had stopped.

Once the equipment was disembarked, they hastened to proceed with the organization of the caravan, and to distribute to the Kabindards, or people of Kabinda, the employments that they were able to fulfill.

Samanou had been appointed *mossenga*—which is to say, chief of the advance guard and enchanter of wild beasts; Dede *djemadar*, or military commander of the caravan's blacks; Kalkali captain of the *Biribis*; Ambacca the chief of the guides; Popo and Congo general overseers of the pagazis recruited in Saint Paul. The latter were divided into brigades of between thirty and forty men, each obedient to a sub-chief responsible to Popo and Congo. Amonquatia had been made flag-bearer, Mimoun instituted as orderly in the tent of the general staff. Finally, Isidore, having had Chocolat set outside the ranks, had attributed him to himself in the capacity of scullion.

On 22 June the caravan had quit Cambambe; on the thirtieth it had arrived at Pedras, a small redoubt situated at 15° east longitude and 9°5 south latitude. It was the last outpost defending the line of the Kwanza, the last barrier opposed by civilization to barbarity. Beyond it, Portuguese influence was only slightly felt.

Having crossed that limit, it was necessary to establish a good operational base. To that effect, Commandant Fresnel had bought a spacious house built in stone, like the European houses in Saint Paul, in a little village extending to the south of Pedras. There he had established a trading post, a provision store, a guesthouse, an infirmary, etc.

Having made these arrangements, the Commandant, essentially intent on only launching forth into the unknown with determined men, had sounded out all his traveling companions one after another. To the irresolute he offered repatriation, still possible while they were at Pedras, the base of operations; to all he declared himself ready to release them from the undertakings made, to tear up all contracts without bitterness.

Isidore having received the mission of questioning Chocolat on that subject, the latter had responded: "*Jurejurando*, Señor Isidore, me *trabandjat* the service *et nunc et semper….*"

"What a fellow! Strong as a Turk. And able to speak English like a Spanish *bufile!*"

"*Dona nobis* of the pancake."

"Oh, of course, after he's done his work, indefatigable for repose and good nourishment! I truly don't know what he has in his belly. Here, you great lump, have a couple of biscuits."

"*Gratias agamus*, Señor Isidore, but you *mirae pitaem nostrum sine condituris…*"

"*Turis?* Ah! *Tu ris!* I don't understand, but I know what you mean. Here, catch these twenty centimeters of sausage, and don't come back too often."

"*Et nunc et semper,*" the mulatto had repeated, hearing his solemn oaths affirmed.

And everyone had expressed intentions in conformity with those of Chocolat.

No one, therefore, took back the word he had given. On the contrary, all of them, Frenchmen and indigenes alike, manifested a vigorous enthusiasm. Monsieur Fresnel, quite satisfied, had therefore been able, on 5 July 1875, to exclaim: "Everything's ready; may God protect us. Let's go! Forward march!"

Chapter XII
The French in the Heart of Africa

On 25 July 1875, therefore, the caravan had quit Pedras to head into the east of Angola, traveling up the right bank of the upper Kwanza.

On the twenty-sixth of September, three months after leaving Pedras, it had reached the pass of Kisala, in the vicinity of Kiboukoue—which is to say, the summit of the mountainous cushion limiting the occidental littoral. A few days after that, on the second of October, it had reached the famous *souk* of Kanika on the oriental slope, the largest market in the region.

There Monsieur Fresnel had obtained from the indigenes the land necessary for the creation of a permanent establishment, a *zeriba*. The expedition's personnel had immediately set to work. Assisted by the Kabindards, the workers had rapidly constructed a large wooden house, outhouses, workshops, storehouses, stables and animal pens: all the accessory buildings that comprise an agricultural exploitation.

The personnel destined for the establishment comprised a station commander, a second in command, a naturalist-physician, a missionary-chaplain, a carpenter, a smith, a weaver and three agriculturists. In accordance with a decision made by Monsieur Fresnel, that first post was named Maizan, in memory of the young ship's ensign, a former pupil of the École Polytechnique who, having made plans to traverse the African continent from east to west in 1845, had been murdered in the Ouzaramo.[30]

At the end of November, the zeriba was finished, provided with a good defensive organization, armed with a cannon and linked to Pedras by a service of indigenous couriers.

Then Commandant Fresnel had judged that he could leave the station of Maizan to itself, permitting it to live its own life in exchange for certain resources left at his disposal.

At the moment when he was preparing, in consequence, to take his leave of the personnel of the zeriba to guide other French colonists eastwards, he had received information that a white voyager had recently passed not far from the frontier of Kinoukoue, that the voyager in question was marching in a direction parallel to the one that the French expedition was following, but that the march in question was being undertaken in the opposite direction.

Who was that European? Captain Harry Fox? No. Commandant Fresnel was to learn later that it was another Englishman, an intrepid officer who, at the price of superhuman efforts, had just traversed the foot of equatorial Africa. That voyager, who would arrive at Saint Paul on 21 November 1875, was Lieutenant Cameron.

On the eighth of December, Commandant Fresnel had said farewell to his friends at Maizan in order to undertake, with the rest of his traveling companions, the descent of the eastern slope of the coastal mountain chain. On 5 February 1876, he had made the acquaintance of the city of Kabebe, situated at 8° 3′ south latitude and 21° 8′ east longitude, and had obtained authori-

---

[30] Eugène Maizan (1816-1845).

zation to colonize a zone on the outskirts of the capital of Oulounda.

They had immediately begun work on the new station. Established on a delightful site on the edge of a wood overlooking an immense savannah, the second French zeriba had been named Le Saint, in memory of a compatriot, a young officer who, departing from Egypt and heading toward Gabon, had died in the Nile Valley on 27 January 1868.[31]

The Le Saint station was endowed with personnel equivalent to that of Maizan. In the last days of March, the establishment was completed, armed with a cannon, linked to Maizan by a corporation of Oulounda couriers, and placed under the special protection of the Mata Yafa, the sovereign of Oulounda.

On 2 April 1876, the personnel of the expedition, already considerably reduced and lightened to the extent of the equipment employed in the organization of the two permanent stations, had quit the zeriba of Le Saint to push forward in an easterly direction. It had crossed the Koné, then the Konn-da-Iroungo, imposing chains of mountains whose system encloses the upper reaches of the Loufira. Having reached the eastern slopes of the Konn-da-Iroungo, it had gone into the region of Oulounda of which the Mata Yafa had delegated the authority to a cazembe, or viceroy.

A third permanent station, similar in all respects to the first two, had been set up on the shore of the little

---

[31] Sub-Lieutenant J. F. M. Le Saint has completely faded from memory, but his expedition is mentioned in the memoirs of Richard Francis Burton, who was also responsible for spreading Maizan's fame with a bloodcurdling account of his murder.

Lake Mofouse. It was called Compiègne, in memory of a young voyager who had come to explore the Ogowe, and who was soon to meet an unfortunate death in Cairo.[32]

On the tenth of August, the caravan had taken its leave of the cazembe, crossed the chain of the Ousango without any obstacle, and then, skirting the frontier of Ilaoua, it had entered into the Ouroungou, the region bathed by the Tanganyika. On the twenty-first of August, after thirteen days of marching, counted from the day they had said farewell to the cazembe, they arrived at Cape Kasohoa, situated on the southern shore of the lake, at 30° east longitude and 7° 20′ south latitude.

At the sight of the admirable equatorial Caspian, a cry of enthusiasm had escaped the throats of all the voyagers, and the negroes of the caravan had responded to it with prolonged hurrahs.

Immediately, Monsieur Fresnel had searched the region of the cape for a tract favorable to the creation of a fourth and final zeriba.

Such reconnaissance had not required long operations; the only difficulty was making a choice between the propitious sites that were offered to the commandant's eyes. Indeed, one cannot imagine anything more beautiful than that region of the Ouroungou: the green valleys that overlook the blue expanse of the Tanganyika from six hundred meters. From Kasoha the view embraces the panorama of the lake, with its splendid shores covered from bottom to top with luxuriant vegetation. One discovers herds of elephants, buffaloes, zebras and antelopes there, coming to drink from the limpid waters populated by hippopotamuses and crocodiles, tumultu-

---

[32] Louis-Alphonse Dupont, Marquis de Compiègne (1846-1877).

ously mingled with multitudes of fish of every species. It really is a terrestrial paradise; as the English put it: "It is as perfect a natural paradise as Xenophon could have desired."

At a very reasonable price, Monsieur Fresnel had made the acquisition of an admirable little valley, opening on to the lake and having for an annex a cove well sheltered from the winds of the open water. They had immediately set to work, and, thanks to the collaboration of the industrious Ouaroundous, the building work had proceeded rapidly. At the end of a month they were approaching their end. The new station was named Debaize, in memory of the courageous missionary who had died at Oujiji on the Tanganyika.[33]

They were, therefore, on the Tanganyika!

A fortunate French expedition had, in the month of September 1876, realized the wishes that were being expressed at that very moment by His Majesty the King of the Belgians. The western coast of the African continent—the coast that prolongs the occidental littoral of old Europe—was connected to the region of the equatorial lakes. The route from Saint Paul de Loanda to the Tanganyika was regularly marked out by the stations of Maizan, Le Saint, Compiègne and Debaize.

The problem was resolved.

The French expedition had spent the months of October and November 1876 at Debaize. It was at precisely that moment that the intrepid Stanley had arrived at Nyangoue, on the Loualaba.

---

[33] This reference is anachronistic, given that Abbé Michel-Alexandre Debaize—who was a Jesuit, but not a missionary—did not die until 1880 and had not yet started for Lake Tanganyika in November 1876, let alone reached it.

Commandant Fresnel had attained his goal and fulfilled all the conditions of the program appended to the testament of Admiral   , the patron of the enterprise. In consequence, he would have been able, without any further peregrinations, to resume the route to Saint Paul. Having fulfilled their duty, and looking over the extent of the success, had brought him certain satisfactions, but he was no longer savoring those legitimate enjoyments. Another ambition had just overtaken him.

"Yes," he said to himself, "I've fulfilled the mission that was confided to me, that's undeniable, and I could, strictly speaking, permit myself an *exegi monumentum*. But what was the foundation of the Admiral's idea? What design had he conceived, if not that of putting across Africa the Atlantic Ocean in communication with the Indian Ocean and the Mediterranean? And why should I, who have traveled and marked out the route from Saint Paul to the Tanganyika, renounce the honor of connecting that section of the route to one of the other sections that is already open? Why not return to France via Oujiji, Bagamoyo and Zanzibar, or even via Albert-Nyanza and the valley of the Nile? I would thus have the glory of having traversed the entire continent, of not having held to the letter but having observed the spirit of the will of the sponsor!"

Nevertheless, Monsieur Fresnel hesitated. He feared imposing on his companions a task and fatigues beyond their strength. But the latter, on being consulted, declared that they were ready to follow him.

Two routes were offered to the French expedition, which would both permit it to complete its return to France, one via the Indian Ocean, the other via the Mediterranean.

They had decided on the latter. They had resolved to traverse the Tanganyika from south to north, and from the northern shore of the lake to the south of the Albert-Nyanza. With a view to that journey, the mechanics had assembled the little steel steamer of which they had the sections; once those elements were assembled, they had a nice ship similar to the *Ilala* that now serves the station of Livingstonia on Lake Nyassa. It was named the *Debaize*, after the fourth zeriba, to which it would belong when it returned. In addition, they had bought from the Ouaroungous one of those crudely fashioned vessels, solidly built, known as *daous*, which would capable of going to sea. A launch drawing about thirty tons completed the French flotilla.

The French had embarked on the twenty-first of November to traverse the lake, which had previously been explored by Burton and Speke, Livingstone, Cameron and Stanley. They had traveled its entire length, from 7° 20′ south latitude to 8° 25′ north latitude—a distance of about four hundred kilometers; comparable, as the English put it, to that of the British coast from Dover to Aberdeen. The extent of the British Isles! Such is the measure of the larger dimension of the lake. Isidore was therefore not mistaken when he deigned to find it considerably superior in extent to the lake in the Bois de Boulogne, and even the bay of Toulon.

On 20 January 1877, after two months of navigation, Monsieur Fresnel, followed by his companions, had gone ashore at Magala, on the northeastern shore of the lake. The following day, the twenty-second of January, he had drawn away from that point in order to go toward Alexandra-Nyanza, a lake of relatively restricted dimensions, which extends between the Albert and the Tanganyika.

In the early days of the march, all went well. The French caravan had only had praise for the conduct of the river dwellers of the Rousizi in their regard. On the twenty-sixth of January, however, as they were entering the first district of the Mkinyaga, the complexion of things had abruptly changed. Taken by surprise by considerable hostile forces, the little troop had been temporarily broken up and dispersed.

Commandant Fresnel, who was marching at the head of the column with the engineer Duvivier, Professor Cornelius, the chaplain Couëdic and Dr. Quentin, had the escort of Biribis close at hand. Nevertheless, and in spite of heroic efforts, he had been cut off from the convoy, which had, as usual, been placed under the surveillance of Isidore, Mimoun and Chocolat.

While the latter had fallen inopportunely into the hands of the attacking hordes, and the ouaroungou porters, gripped by panic, had unceremoniously abandoned the baggage that had been confided to them, the general staff, supported by the Biribis—to whom Samanou, Amonquatia and Popo had rallied—had at first opposed a frank and solid resistance to the aggressors. Soon, however, fearing, not without reason, that they would be surrounded and overrun if they stayed where they were, they had made the decision to beat a retreat and return to the northern extremity of Lake Tanganyika.

After four days of incessant combats and great dangers, the French had been fortunate enough to find a refuge in the banza of Kisimbasimba, into which the people of the surrounding region had retreated at the same time.

This is how Cornelius gave Isidore an account of that last episode.

"That horde of negroes," he said, "that diabolical army, as you so aptly call it, was sowing fire and blood throughout the valley of the Rousizi; populations maddened by terror were fleeing at first sight of them. The city that we're occupying was doubtless a refuge prepared long ago for the pursued peasants, for its barriers were urgently lowered when they approached, and the doors were opened wide. Then the whole crowd of the worthy people precipitated themselves into the place…and we followed them. We simply entered pell-mell with them on the thirtieth of January."

"But where are they, then, these townspeople?" Isidore put in.

"That's what we've never been able to discover."

"What? Aren't they here any longer?"

"No."

"Strange! They've gone away, then?"

"No, for we're the ones who have guarded the gates; we're the ones who've shut ourselves in, and since that famous day they haven't re-opened; we're perfectly certain of that."

"Ah! I've got it. They're clever—they came right through the city at a run; they decamped via the lake."

"No, the bottleneck is closed by a boom that's already covered with a thick mass of algae and mollusks; the construction of that device, in wood, was certainly anterior to our arrival here, as Monsieur Duvivier has demonstrated very clearly. In any case, all the vessels, rafts, canoes or daous, are still moored there in the harbor, where you can see them."

"But in the end, Monsieur, what do you think has happened to the crowd? Oh, I see…they've gone to ground in their ruined antiquities."

"You think they're in these old edifices? Wrong. They've all been carefully searched several times. We haven't found anything. We've called out; our guides have shouted words of peace at the top of their voice; no one has responded."

"So, they came in, no one has seen them go out, but they're no longer here? No one knows what's become of them?"

"That's right."

"Well, it's a bit stiff! But, after all, I've seen such funny things recently that, in truth, if someone were to tell me that these jokers have flown away over the walls like cockchafers, or eclipsed themselves like the moon, or vanished like cigar smoke... whoever told me that... well, no, Monsieur, I wouldn't pass my skewer through his body; I wouldn't send him to lie down in the tent; I wouldn't even tell him to tell it to Plumeau—you know Plumeau, the zouaves' wig maker, who tells so many tall stories! I'd simply reply to him: My friend, there's no need to fatigue your memory or rack your temperament any longer; everything that you say there is a bit stiff...but it's possible. I can't say better than that."

Chapter XIII
A Council of War

It was the twenty-eighth of March. It would soon be a month that a handful of Europeans had been holding firmly at bay the forces of an army of savages. Without improving the situation greatly, the return of Isidore might perhaps occasion modifications in the general nature of the defense. The zouave-cook, who had just presided over the operations of the attack in the capacity of commanding general, could, at any rate, supply useful information. Given that, Monsieur Fresnel thought that he ought to hold a council of war.

He assembled his companions in the shade of a palm tree, under a hut affecting an octagonal form, atop the soil of which was covered with a thick layer of goat dung. Such is, in those latitudes, the only means one has of protecting oneself against the attacks of the large ferocious ants that, in order better to bite a traveler and suck his blood, stick their entire head under his skin. A flagpole bearing the French colors was planted in front of the hut.

The members of the council presided over by the Commandant were engineer Duvivier, Professor Cornelius Bernard and Dr. Quentin. Abbé Le Couëdic, the mechanic, the smith and the carpenter represented the audience.

"Isidore Chauvelot," called the Commandant, opening the session.

"Present!"

"You left the ranks of the column on 26 January 1877. It's now the twenty-eighth of March. You have, therefore, been absent without leave for more than two months."

"Two months! Well, it seemed longer than that to me."

"I invite you to abstain from all useless or unhealthy reflections. In the course of that period of absence you accepted the command of a body of indigenous troops."

"Yes, Commandant, that's true.

"You, a French subject, have, without the authorization of your government, which I represent here, entered the service of a foreign power."

"Those people were, in fact, strangers to me."

"Please remain silent; let me establish the facts. At the head of these troops, which you describe yourself as 'the diabolical army,' you fought against us."

"Oh! Commandant, I didn't know…."

"I know what you can allege, for your defense; the court will take that into account. It understands that the circumstances in which you found yourself were exceptional; but it is nevertheless an established fact that you've borne arms against your fatherland. Do you admit that?"

"I can't deny it, Commandant."

"That's good; stand down. The council will deliberate."

Having saluted militarily, Isidore left the hut and went tranquilly to smoke a cigarette a short distance away. Hardened by the events that had taken place during those two months, he was quite calm.

After a quarter of an hour, hearing himself summoned, he returned with a firm tread, making the military salute once again. The members of the council of war were standing up.

"Isidore Chauvelot," said the president, "the facts being incontestable and the terms of the law being precise...." At this point, Monsieur Fresnel's voice caught in his throat. He had to pause.

It was the accused who went on: "Have no fear of continuing, Commandant. I'm used to all this, now that I spend my life being condemned to death."

"Yes, unanimously, the council of war has been obliged to pronounce the death penalty against you. Have you anything to say regarding that sentence?"

"No, Commandant. It needs to end. I'd rather settle my account here than among the savages. I'd like my dozen bullets right away, and if you're prepared to be generous, I'll give the order to fire."

"That's good."

"Let's proceed!"

"Isidore, the council that has just condemned you has presented a plea for mercy on your behalf."

"Ah!"

"And that mercy I grant."

"Commandant! Oh well, what do you want me to say? That doesn't astonish me, on your part. But if it's any inconvenience, don't bother. Me, I've seen enough lately that it's all the same to me to get it over with. Sooner or later, it'll still be necessary to die here."

Isidore made as if to withdraw, but the Commandant said: "The session isn't concluded; I invite you to remain at the disposal of the court."

"It's not finished, then? Do you also want to settle Mimoun's account, or even poor Chocolat's? Are you going to judge them?"

"No," said the president, without any malice. "We're only going to judge the situation."

"The situation? Well, I like that better."

"Messieurs," said Commandant Fresnel, "you know what the extraordinary situation is. We have, by virtue of a providential circumstance, found refuge in a fortress admirably organized for resistance, whose natural defenders have abandoned it since we arrived here in an incomprehensible fashion. Our resources, you know; a singularly reduced personnel has nevertheless permitted us, thus far, to keep thousands of barbarians at bay."

"Thousands, Commandant! You could say hordes— oh yes, diabolical hordes!"

"So be it. In the matter of materiel, it's necessary to distinguish. We possess food in considerable quantities; we'll never exhaust the immense storehouses and abundant granaries staked up under this species of Capitol that dominates the city. The inhabitants, now disappeared, have been taking their precautions for a long time and have gathered extraordinary provisions here; thus, we have at our discretion manioc, yams, maize, sorghum, ground nuts, beans, smoked fish, eland fat and eleusine beer. We have countless parks cluttered with animals, packed with livestock of every kind, and we don't have to nourish those herds...."

"What! Not nourish them!" interrupted Isidore, sharply. "For after all, unless they can live on fresh air...."

"It's strange, indeed, and none of us has yet been able to penetrate the mystery. What is certain is that the animals are in good condition, and that we don't occupy ourselves with their subsistence, which is abundantly provided without our knowing how."

"Commandant, you can speak without fear. Personally, I'll believe anything you want now. I've seen so much in such a short time that, word of honor, nothing can astonish me anymore."

"On the other hand, Messieurs, in the matter of munitions, our means are extremely limited. On the twenty-sixth of January, cut off from our convoy, we lost our baggage. When it was necessary to beat a retreat, we carried away what we had on hand or on our persons, our garments and our weapons. During that retreat we had to fire more often than we'd have liked to, with the result that we now have only a few cartridges left. In that regard, we're in such deprivation that, if we had had to put Isidore before a firing squad, conceding him the dozen bullets to which he had the right...."

"Oh, as to that, of course, Commandant, I wouldn't have let you off. I've been a soldier; I want to end as a soldier. I've had enough of being tied to trees or stuffed into conjuror's bags."

"Your rights are undeniable; but be certain that, in granting you mercy, I was consulting justice rather than economy."

"The Commandant is great and generous; I've said it before and I repeat it—that doesn't astonish me on his part. I, too, am just...but honest. I wouldn't have cost my comrades anything. Look, Commandant, here's eighty of them—cartridges, that is. I had four packets of twenty in my pockets. I'll let you have them. Which proves once more that virtue is always rewarded, as Boileau says."

"Thank you, Isidore. That contribution of ammunition is precious, but we ought to think of it as a reserve supply, on which we ought only to draw in case of absolute necessity, as a last resort. Let's reason, therefore, setting aside that unexpected help. Until now, Messieurs, only having an extremely limited number of men, we acted on the principle of concealing from the enemy the totality of that insignificant number. We've kept out of sight, hidden; we've tried to act vigorously while remaining invisible. What do you think, Isidore? Is it a reasonable system?"

"Oh, I think it's very good. Those brigands aren't very clever; they think the city here at present is inhabited by spirits. They must be stupid."

"Then it's probably appropriate to continue that policy; the council will decide. On the other hand, Messieurs, we have not thus far made use of our firearms, for lack of munitions. In that situation, we ought to reckon ourselves fortunate to have been able to make use of several neuroballistic devices analogous to those employed by the ancients. The idea was Monsieur Cornelius Bernard's. To Monsieur Duvivier reverts the honor of having rapidly realized that conception. He has been able to improvise an excellent field artillery for us. Let's see Isidore, what do you think of our lithoboles?"

"Litho...? Don't know."

"We also have trebuchets, as in the Middle Ages."

"Oh yes, the Middle Ages...the time of the great Frederick. But why make trebuchets? Doubtless to catch sparrows?"

"No, lithoboles and trebuchets are machines that serve to launch stones in the guise of cannonballs."

"Ah! Of course, that's excessively engineerious! Can you imagine that when they fall to earth, those big stones make a *pouff!* And then, men crushed, as you like, and there you are! No doubt about it; it's very engineerious. And do you know what they say, those Cossacks in the diabolical army? They think those pebbles and other trinkets are falling on them from the sky! If that doesn't make you split your sides…!"

"In any case, it will doubtless be a good idea to continue with that sort of bombardment. You can formulate an opinion in that regard. Finally, Messieurs, for want of a garrison, having neither troops nor men that we can make into soldiers, we've had recourse to auxiliary combatants. Another of Monsieur Cornelius' ideas. Given our absolute penury of human beings, we've sent forth animals. For lack of bipeds, we've launched at the enemy columns those quadrupeds of all species that are nourished by a mysterious hand, and of which the enchanter Samanou has made such good use. What do you think, Isidore? Our buffaloes and our lions, for example—were they effective?"

"Yes, Commandant, that's the bouquet. One can even say that it's a rude invention. I know something about it, me! My compliments to Samanou."

"Well, Messieurs, that being so, and Isidore having measured the value of our original methods by experience, I must ask you whether you don't judge it useful to remain faithful to them—and whether it might not be opportune to continue our work with redoubled effort, operation on a large scale."

"A big ladder!" muttered Isidore.[34] "They're crazy, word of honor. It would be as easy for Monsieur Duvivier to make us elevators, like the ones at the Grand Hotel!"

While the cook was grumbling in that fashion about the routine intelligence of the engineer, the council decidedly unanimously that it would not bring any kind of

---

[34] Isidore has misconstrued the expression *grand échelle*, which can mean both "large scale" and "big ladder."

modification to the system of defense operated thus far; that it would on the contrary, persevere with it, making the most of its effects, and would do so until they had exhausted its last consequences."

With that, the session was closed.

While the members of the council headed for lunch, the former ganga-ya-ita took Professor Cornelius to one side.

"So," he said, "it was that joker Samanou who threw beasts at me?"

"Yes.

"That's clever! So it was him who cut off their tails?"

"Yes, of course."

"But why?"

"To render them furious. The effects of ablation of the caudal appendage are well known. Animals that no longer have a tail scream, howl and roar."

"Ah! I understand—and I promise you that Samanou's affair succeeded very well. Those lions put on an infernal sabbat for us!"

Chapter XIV
Forty-Seven Men against Five Hundred Thousand

The next day, Commandant Fresnel, having gathered all his traveling companions together, not for a council of war, but simply in conference, thought he ought to call upon Isidore once again.

"You can render us another service," he told him.

"At your orders, Commandant. What do I have to do?"

"Appeal to your memories in order to give us precise information about the means that the people besieging us have at their disposal. Let me interrogate you. You inspected the lake squadron. Do you know how large it is?"

"Oh, it's very consequent."

"You've seen it at close range and visited the boats? How many are there. How big? What armaments to they have?"

"First of all, Commandant, there are a lot of little dinghies, each manned by two men; the number one holds the paddle and the number two the assegai—I remembered that because it's funny.[35] Some of those dinghies look like little canoes, and others make one think of the raft of the *Medusa*. I didn't count them, of course, but there were fleets, perhaps a thousand."

"That already makes two thousand men, then?"

"At least. Secondly—these I counted, there were eighty-two—canoes made from a single block of wood,

---

[35] Isidore thinks it's funny because in French, *pagaie* [paddle] rhymes with *sagaie* [assegai].

which are long…two or three times as long as the *Bia-fra*'s lifeboat. There might have been a hundred and twenty-five or a hundred and thirty men in each one."

"Which makes about ten thousand men in total."

"That's not all. There are also boats like the one in which we passed over the lake."

"Daous?"

"Precisely. There are twenty-four; one can say that they're the real warships; each one has its forty oars, its thirty able seamen, its hundred and twenty fighting men, archers, and riflemen, and drummers…oh, what drummers!"

"That makes, by that count, about three hundred men aboard each daou."

"About that."

And as the fleet comprises twenty-four of those ships, we have another seven thousand men there. Is that all?"

"Yes, commandant, that's all; but I can tell you that it's very consequent, without seeming like it. Those dinghies, those big canoes, even those huge daous, you won't see them all. Not so stupid as all that, those matelots! They're in ambush in all the little corners of the coast, behind the islets or under the rocks that stick out, or in forests of reeds."

"In sum, Messieurs, according to Isidore's account, we're blockaded on the lake by naval forces whose strength can be drawn up as follows: crews of little boats, two thousand men; canoes, ten thousand; daous, seven thousand—which is, in total, about twenty thousand men. Now the land forces, what number would you put on their strength?"

"Commandant, the land armies, that's my game, since I was in the zouaves. Well, all those men there are lousy soldiers. They're not worth much—devilishly little. On the other hand, there are *masses*. There in front of you, those who are blockading us, is the Kifoukourou camp, a corps of at least seventy thousand men. Half a day from here is the Nyonngo camp; at least another seventy thousand men. Well, Commandant, I heard it from the Mata Sonapanga that he had seven like that—army corps, that is—within a few days march. That's it."

"What! We're blockaded by an army of four hundred and fifty thousand men!"

"That's what I make it. And that's not all. There are the women in the train, the tringlotes; there are the elephants...sixty in each corps, each with four men on its back and a driver on its neck."

"Which makes another two or three thousand men. In sum, Messieurs, if Isidore is to be believed, we're at odds with an enemy whose land and water-borne forces add up to approximately half a million men—but to tell the truth, that seems to me to be fabulous."

"Why?" demanded Professor Cornelius. "Such a number is well in accordance with historical data. Carli relates that he saw a certain king of the Congo marching against the Portuguese one day at the head of an army of more than nine hundred thousand men. Pigafetta thought that he ought to add that the king in question normally had more than a million under arms; that in 1584 the Portuguese had to sustain the attack of twelve hundred thousand negroes in Angola.[36] Those figures aren't ex-

---

[36] The Capuchin friar Denis de Carli undertook a journey to the Congo in 1666-67. Filippo Pigafetta had published an account of the kingdoms of the Congo even earlier, in 1591, which included a historically significant map.

aggerated. Extreme barbarism proceeds, like extreme civilization, in vast masses."

"So be it," Monsieur Fresnel resumed. "Let's admit the figure of five hundred thousand men; I ought to ask you to consider that they're not all here, those half million combatants—that the nine army corps haven't yet joined up."

"Commandant," said Isidore, firmly, "you can take it as certain that it won't take long."

"How do you know?"

"I heard the Mata say so on the evening when I had the sack from my feet to my ears....and even over my head. He was furious to see that I hadn't been able to take the city. Then, before beginning to drink the pommbé with his generals and his big bassoons, he gave the order to have all of them summoned here—and he even said that, if the nine army corps weren't sufficient, he'd call up the reserves of all classes from back in his homeland: that if it took a hundred and sixty-nine corps, he'd end up victorious. Oh, he's stubborn, that young man. His obsession is to take Kisimbasimba."

"What's Kisimbasimba?" asked Monsieur Fresnel.

"The city where we are, so I believe. Anyway, he said that he'd take it; he swore it by Ouaka. That's the name of the chief of the spirits of his homeland."

"Ouaka!" interjected Professor Cornelius. "You say that their god is called Ouaka?"

"Certainly, saving your respect."

"Then we're not dealing with Nyam-Nyams, as I thought at first, but with the Galla."

"No, that's not what they call themselves."

"Orma, if you wish."

"Orma—yes, that's it."

133

"That's the national name, which signifies 'strong men.' We Europeans call them the Galla—which is to say, 'emigrants.' Tell me, Isidore, do you know how long it's been since they left their homeland, how long they've been on the move?"

"The Mata claims that it's been five years—the same time as an enlistment, but I can't believe...."

"Wait! With the African year only being five months, it will merely be two years that these people have been marching. Did you hear talk of the land they inhabit? Did their conversation include the names of Mount Kenia or Kilimanjaro, the river Juba or the river Sabaki?"

"Sabaki! Yes—I remembered that name because it's funny."

"Well, now I'm sure of it—they're Galla from the south. So much the worse!"

"What do you mean?" asked Monsieur Fresnel.

"That Isidore doubtless had under his command combatants that don't constitute elite troops; that those people probably experienced some repugnance at serving under the orders of an *ousoungou*; either they were troubled by the idea of having to lay siege to a banza, or they were demoralized by virtue of the character of our defensive method—but I declare that it would be difficult for us to encounter more redoubtable adversaries."

"What!"

"Yes, we have at our heels the most bellicose of all the peoples of the African continent, not excepting the Zulus.

"The Zuzus?" Isidore queried.

"I said Zulus. One ought to say: Oulus, which signifies 'the devil's people.' It's a nation of the cape, much superior to those of the Kaffirs, Hottentots, Basutos and

Fingas. The English, who praise the Zulu highly, say that he's very distinguished in all things: 'every inch a gentleman.' What's certain is that the people of Zululand are truly astonishing. Indefatigable marchers, they move on the double for twenty-four hours in succession, taking the shortest route, never resting, eating or drinking. One would willingly grant them the gift of ubiquity. Armed with hardwood assegais with iron points, they launch those javelins over long distances, and with extraordinary accuracy. In a word, they're true warriors. The English know that one day, something…well, the Galla that we have to fight are even more terrible than the people of the Cape."

"We beg you to tell us all that you know about this enemy that you claim to be so terrible. It's good to know what one's dealing with."

"All right, you'll learn what the Galla are—but first, there are a few general considerations of which I ought to make you aware. I beg your pardon—just a little ethnography! It won't take long. Without going into detail about the presumed truth of prehistoric migrations, I should remind you that the African continent is occupied today by populations that can be divided, as Monsieur Keane[37] has done, into six distinct races. Of those six races, two are of foreign origin and four autochthonous, or indigenous.

"The foreigners are the Chamitic race and the Semitic race, today almost exclusively inhabiting the north and northeast of the continent. The autochthonous races are the Negroes properly speaking, the Fulani, the Bantus and the Hottentots. The Blacks occupy the central

---

[37] The ethnologist Augustus Henry Keane (1833-1912), who published his racial theories in *Nature* in 1879-81.

zone, which extends from the Atlantic to the Egyptian Sudan. The Fulani are established in the northwest of the continent; the Bantus occupy the entire south, from a few degrees below the equator to the Cape, except for a few corners of the extreme south and the extreme southwest, which together constitute the domain of the Hottentots. Such is the present distribution of the races on the surface of the African continent.

"The Chamitic race, the only one that I need to deal with, probably originated in southwest Asia, in the Savannah countries bathed by the Tigris and the Euphrates. The epoch of its arrival in Africa is lost in the night of time. It has formed three distinct families: the Egyptian, Libyan and Ethiopian families.

"Having said that, what is the origin of the Galla? According to their own traditions, they came from Arabia. Some ethnographic fantasists find affinities with the Kaffirs, others with the Galla negroes that inhabit Guinea between Cap Mesurado and the Pepper coast. Speke took them for hybrids of Negroes and Abyssinians. Personally, I'm content to say that the Galla are Chamites of the Ethiopian family.

"There's no need to sketch the type of our adversaries; Isidore has done that. He has depicted the Galla who, physically, occupy a good rank in the scale of races. His description is in conformity with those given by Rudolf, Bruce, Salt, Owen, Lefevre Hoefer, Desvergers and, very recently, Keith Johnson, a member of the Royal Geographical Society of London.[38] I will add that

---

[38] Alexander Keith Johnson F.R.G.S. published a guide to physical geography intended for use in schools in 1869. He published a much more detailed book specifically about Africa in 1884, which Hennebert might have seen before the Mame

they're very intelligent, and no more proof of that is needed than the fact that a few Galla tribes can read and write; they make use of old Ethiopian characters, and we possess a curious specimen of that writing brought back by Arnaud d'Abbadie.[39] It's a letter from the Galla King of Enaria addressed to an Abyssinian prince.

"Always following their national traditions, the Galla might once have possessed all of Central Africa. At any rate, Barth is right to attribute to them as a base of operations and a primary fatherland the region where Kilimanjaro rises. It's certain that they've occupied since remote antiquity the eastern coast that extends south of Abyssinia. It's even thought that their name has been recognized in the famous inscription of Adulis among the names of the people whose submission was obtained by the Ptolemies.

"As for the territory that they possess today, we know its limits almost exactly, thanks to Rebmann, Wakefield, von der Decken, Krapf, Charles New and Keith Johnson. That territory is limited to the north by Abyssinia; to the east by the land of the Somalis, following a straight line leading from the bay of Tajurra on the gulf of Aden to the mouth of the Juba in the Indian Ocean; to the south by the course of the Sabaki and the plateau of the Ouanika; to the southwest by the Ouakambani, who live between the Kenia and Kiliman-

---

edition of his novel was published, but the reference is probably based on the earlier text, from which the preceding and subsequent lists of names are likely to have been appropriated.
[39] Arnaud-Michel d'Abbadie and his brother Antoine travelled widely in what is now Ethiopia between 1838 and 1848, to which Arnaud returned in 1853. Arnaud published *Douze ans dans la Haute-Ethiopie* in 1868.

jaro; to the west by the Oumasai and the Ouakouavi, brigand peoples who perpetually ravage the plains that extend from Abyssinia to the great lakes. The immense patrimony of the Galla thus designs, between the tenth degree of north latitude and the fourth degree of south latitude, a zone fifteen hundred kilometers in extent. That long strip of territory is scarcely populated as it might be; Dr. Krapf[40] only estimates the total population at six or eight million inhabitants.

"As regards their political organization, the Galla follow a kind of patriarchal regime; divided into a considerable number of tribes and clans, they recognize the authority, albeit rather limited, of a helitch or sultan. This Mata Sonapanga about whom Isidore has talked to us is only a generalissimo invested with a military dignity equivalent to that of a French maréchal. He has been elected under the tree of war. The sovereign resides in a capital called Bizamo or Killambanza, situated between the Nile and the Bahr-el-Abiad, which no European has yet visited. The Galla of the north, those bordering on Abyssinia, have some trace of civilization; some of them are Muslims, others Christians. Those of the south are pagans; they worship Ouaka, a supreme being whose attributes are in reasonable harmony with the ideas that civilized peoples have of the divinity."

"All that's very interesting, my dear professor—but let's talk about the military institutions of the people we have to fight."

"The Galla are to Africa what the Goths and Vandals once were to Western Europe. They scarcely make

---

[40] The linguist Johann Ludwig Krapf travelled widely in Africa, latterly in the company of Johannes Rebmann, between 1843 and 1853.

use of agriculture, but they tend a few herds. Their cattle are remarkable because of their immensely long horns. Above all, they are, like the Fans or Pahouins, pirates of the land, savage warriors, devastators. Their great-armed expeditions are nearly periodic, like the inundations of the Nile, but instead of bringing fecundity, they spread death and desolation wherever they go.

"For four hundred years they've been ravaging the regions of the equatorial lakes. In the sixteenth century, in 1537, they invaded Abyssinia, a few years later, Angola and the Congo. Today they're dominant in Kittara, Ourinza, Kragoue, Ouganda and Ounioro; yesterday, they were on the borders of Victoria-Nyanza; now, they're here in the Tanganyika. The city that we're occupying commands the roads that lead in a westerly direction; it's the key to the passages that they have to effect, in accordance with the law of ethnological currents that is drawing them toward the western coast."

"You think that they won't turn back—that they won't renounce their enterprise?"

"Oh, no. It's necessary to them, this banza that we're occupying. They doubtless know that; they know that it encloses considerable resources. For them it's an indispensable storehouse, a strategic point that they can't bypass. Isidore is right—these people are extraordinarily stubborn; tenacity is the dominant quality of their character. Once attached to the prey that they covet, they don't let go. It's impossible to distract them. They never retreat, save for one circumstance—that in which they lose the chief commanding them, their Mata Sonapanga. Then, everything is finished; they admit defeat and disperse in the greatest disorder. In the meantime, they'll return to the charge; we can expect them to come."

"Very good," said Fresnel. "We have at hand an army of five hundred thousand men, and, in order to face up to that immense horde, we are, in total, forty-seven! Messieurs, let's prepare the resistance!"

Chapter XV
An Improvised Armament

By the following morning, that of the twenty-ninth of March, Commandant Fresnel had drawn up a series of energetic measures, the only ones from which they had any right to expect a means of salvation. He had conferred for a long time with the engineer Duvivier and Professor Cornelius, the members of the general staff of an army reduced to forty-seven defenders.

"This is what we've agreed," he said, summarizing the conversation. You, Monsieur Duvivier, say that you need a fortnight's uninterrupted work, and you promise to be ready within that interval—so be it. But don't ask me for one minute more; I sense that it will be impossible for me to give it to you. You, Monsieur Cornelius, while our engineer's time will be absorbed by his new duties, will take charge of his ordinary service, which you'll carry out concurrently with your own. You'll have the direction of the neurotonic artillery and also the combat menagerie.

"Now, Messieurs, let each of us go to his post! I have no need to recommend you to activity and vigilance, but I call your attention to the necessity of operating in the greatest secrecy. The enemy is observing us; there might be spies among our pagazis; it would be easy for them to discover our plans. So let's not breathe a word of the plans we've just made!"

With that, they separated.

Commandant Fresnel went to his observatory, a kind of hut or sentry box that he had established at the summit of a small pyramid that overlooked the upper city. One could see from there not only the terrain of attacks but also the perimeter of the location.

Monsieur Duvivier went down to the harbor with the two mechanics, the carpenter, the smith and the Kabindards,

Professor Cornelius, accompanied by the Biribis and the mossenga Samanou, headed for the section of the ramparts that overlooked the camp of Kifoukourou.

At about midday, Isidore, following the orders he had received, brought everyone their daily rations.

"The Commandant is served," he said, after having deposited the various elements of a summary lunch on the little table that supplied, along with a bench, the entire furniture of the observatory.

Monsieur Fresnel did not seem to have heard. He was aiming his telescope at the surrounding country and interrogating the horizon with an anxious expression.

"The Commandant is served," Isidore repeated.

"Ah!" said Monsieur Fresnel, finally. "Well, I believe you're right; I seem to perceive troops arriving in large numbers. If my eyes aren't deceiving me, they'll be within rifle shot before nightfall."

"What did I tell you?"

"It would have been better for all of us if you'd been mistaken."

"That's my opinion, too, Commandant."

From the observatory, Isidore went down to the shore in order to take food to the engineer and his crew of artisans.

The quays of the little harbor now offered the aspect of an abattoir, cluttered as they were with the cadavers of animals. Seven or eight buffalo, three rhinoceroses, a dozen hippopotamuses and an elephant were

142

lying on the ground. The Kabindards were skinning them, butchering them and emptying them out. It was hideous. The cook felt sick.

Swiftly, he deposited the provisions destined for Monsieur Duvivier on the shore, and hastened back to the post occupied by Professor Cornelius.

There, everything was calm. The professor and his men were manifesting neither the anguish of an observer struggling against the evidence of a grave circumstance, the indication of an imminent catastrophe, nor the feverish activity of a band of butchers working up to their elbows in blood with a view to some abominable project.

The professor did honor to the lunch; he did not refuse, while eating, to reply to the cook's questions, and, given that the latter served him fine dishes, the affability of his responses testified to his gratitude.

""How odd all this is!" Isidore said to him. "It's unbelievable, all the things that happen here! There are things that surpass me. Can you imagine, for example, that the evening when I arrived at the city with a detachment of the diabolical army, a vile multitude of mice chewed up my men's weapons and equipment? Was it by chance, then, that they did that?"

"Probably not, and it's explicable. The habitual occupants of the city we're now occupying doubtless planted those myriads of little creatures systematically, at a good distance—by which I mean in such a manner as to hinder the enemy's investment operations. You had the bad idea to take up a position on top of the *Oum-et-Firan*, as the Arabs put it—the city of mice—and paid the penalty."

"Now, that's funny. I understand...."

"Console yourself, anyway—you're not the first to whom such an accident has happened. Such events aren't unknown in history. Once, a king of Egypt was able to paralyze in that fashion an invading army commanded by the famous Sennacherib, king of Assyria, one of the successors of Sardanapolis."

"Sardanapolis! Of, yes, under the Regency...."

"A little earlier than that, in fact."

"Oh, a little sooner, a little later, what does it matter to me now that I know I'm not the first general to fall into the mouse-trap? But tell me, Monsieur—those honey flies that stung us, was it the inhabitants who sent them after us?"

"No, but they were the ones who facilitated their entrance onto the stage. Africa is rich in insects of that sort, to the extent that the ancients named it Kephenia—the land of wasps. Instead of letting them wander the region, the inhabitants prepared fixed dwellings for them, to the effect of supporting the weak points in their ramparts. Didn't you see them? Look at all those beehives lined up behind the palisade and the wooden stockade. You had the unfortunate idea of setting fire to it, and, well—the bees saw red."

"Oh, yes—as red as the blood they took from us. But with regard to the fire, who set the fires in the fields on the day of the lions' fantasia? My men said that the flames came out of the city, and I saw them myself, flying like shooting stars."

"You, you're right, the fires came from the besieged city, and they certainly ought to have flown swiftly, for on my instigation, we had recourse to the method inaugurated by Samson."

"Samson! The executioner?"

"Not exactly. I mean the Samson in the Bible—the one who burned the Philistines' crops with the aid of animate pyrophores."

"Pyrophores! That must be powerful stuff. What is it?"

"Three hundred foxes, to which the judge of Israel attached flaming torches. The mossenga Samanou operated in accordance with the same principle, with the difference that instead of foxes he used other animal incendiaries: wolves, elands and others antelopes."

"A good trick, in fact! They nearly roasted me. That joker Samanou!"

Having finished his lunch, the professor, who had to make a tour of inspection of the sectors for which he was respectable, took Isidore with him, to whom he gave a few explanations on the spot.

"We haven't had to make all the dispositions ourselves whose ensemble constitutes the defensive system," he told him. "The inhabitants of the city, incessantly exposed to the danger of invasions, took precautions long ago against the barbarians whose character seems to me to be permanent. Always on their guard, they kept wild beasts in the dry ditches of the enclosure, crocodiles in the moats full of water, guard-ibises on the ramparts that know when to cry out, like the geese of the Capitol, and, at the foot of the wall, elephants trained to serve as sentries and door keepers, like the one that took you prisoner and invited you to come in.

"It's also the inhabitants who organized all the accessory defenses that you can see: shells, caltrops, little spikes with fire-hardened points, networks of cords, wolf traps—or, more precisely, leopard traps—clusters of elephant tusks, and a thousand other ingenious measures. What they haven't invented, and which is credited to our own initiative, is the ballistic apparatus that hurled projectiles of all kinds at you: bronze ingots, blocks of stone or statues, bombs filled with rats, flaming arrows or darts circled by venomous snakes. Look, here they are, the engines in question, analogous to those you might have seen in the Musée de Saint-Germain.

"The operation is due to the force of torsion of several bundles of elastic fibers, made from buffalo hide, which exercise their action on the propulsive levers, like the cord of a saw that maintains its tightening screw. You might call it a renewal of Greek artillery, for antiquity was familiar with weapons of that sort, which were distinguished into catapults, balistas, onagers, scorpions, etc.

"The catapults constructed here by Monsieur Duvivier can launch weights of one kilogram three hundred meters. Our lithobolic onager can send two-kilogram stones two hundred and fifty meters. It only requires two men to maneuver one of the engines. Our Biribis, commanded by Popo, perform the function of artillerymen, which is new to them, marvelously.

"To become expert in the art of making power talk, the first necessity is to have some. We didn't have any, so we had to make do with what we had. That's what we did!"

The professor did not conceal his satisfaction. His neuroballistic equipment was in good condition; the devices functioned perfectly. Each of the batteries, all well-hidden from the sight of the besiegers, were ready to fire; the operators were showing an indomitable zeal.

Later that the afternoon, Isidore went back to the kitchens. That evening, at dinnertime, he repeated his tour of the posts to the general staff.

Professor Cornelius was radiant. Monsieur Duvivier seemed preoccupied, even though the first day's labor had realized successes. An enormous quantity of raw materials had been amassed on the docks of the harbor:

skins, grease, ropes made of aloe and animal guts, wood of various species and elephant tusks; a multitude of various objects had been accumulated with a view to being imminently put to work.

Commandant Fresnel came down from his observatory. He said, gravely, to Isidore: "Unfortunately, you weren't mistaken. Tomorrow, a flood of invaders will be battering the foot of our walls."

Chapter XVI
New Procedures in the Art
of Defending Strongholds

Indeed, on the thirtieth of March, the stronghold defended by a handful of Europeans had to contend with the pressure of a host of barbarians forming a circle around its perimeter of considerable thickness. From his observatory, Commandant Fresnel was able to follow all the movements of the forces thus concentrated.

He watched the general headquarters of the newly gathered army being installed on a mound situated in advance of Kifoukourou. A lance with a pennon of black ostrich plumes was planted in the earth; a crimson standard floated atop the shaft. At the foot of the lance, a seated man presided over an assembly of some fifty old men. Isidore, having applied his eye to the telescope, was able to affirm to the Commandant that the man was indeed the Mata Sonapanga, that he was sitting on a stool, and that the stool was made of bronze.

The Galla spent the whole day of the thirtieth of March deliberating. Obviously, they were taking up positions on the terrain before launching the surge that would be necessary to overwhelm the impudent fortress, otherwise inaccessible to the terror that their arms sowed everywhere.

It was, on the contrary, the defense that dealt the first thrust of astonishment to the besiegers. At nightfall, Monsieur Duvivier hoisted two mannequins onto the ramparts designed to serve as scarecrows. One, looking toward Kifoukourou, represented a colossal lion, and the other, turned toward the lake, an enormous crocodile. Those animal phantoms had been constructed the day before on the instructions of Monsieur Cornelius. The savant professor had related to the council of defense the story of the wooden elephants once fabricated by Semiramis, and that of the fantastic dragons that garnished the walls of Peking during the French expedition. He had recalled the effect produced during the last war by the batteries that the Prussians had organized with the aid of plows and stove pipes.

Each of Monsieur Duvivier's mock-ups was composed of a light wooden carcass covered with thin skins; inside, a large lantern was burning, whose wick was fueled by brightly burning eland grease. From his observatory, Monsieur Fresnel was able to judge the effect; the illusion was complete. Isidore thought that he was able to assure his master that the optical illusion would produce serious results, that the Galla would talk more than ever about the spirits of the lake, and that the morale of the troops would be affected by it.

Indeed, as soon as the lanterns were lit, confused tumultuous cries erupted from all the sectors of the camp; uneasy rumors persisted for as long as the illumination lasted.

The next day, the thirty-first of March, the besiegers, doubtless shaken, remained inactive and immobile. Another day gained: a day of which the engineer's workshops did not fail to take advantage.

The alarm that the luminous monsters had inspired could not be eternal, however. At daybreak on the first of April, a party of assailants did not hesitate to attempt a surprise attack. A few determined Galla, having broken the first palisade, aimed at a point of the enclosure that they assumed to be poorly guarded precisely because of its defensive value, because they could see that it was protected by a ditch filled with water. Having silently crossed over by boat, they tried to attach to the wall one of the long liana ropes used in Africa by parrot hunters. Popo was watching with his Biribis, however; at a given moment, they sent a rain of heavy objects down on the bold Galla: lumps of bronze, lead "salmon," iron "dolphins" and blocks of stone, suspended from the top of the wall with the aid of thin cords, which it was sufficient for them to cut at the opportune moment. The ladder was broken and the enemy crushed.

Professor Cornelius was right to say that the enemy was singularly tenacious. Without being disturbed by that first check, other Galla followed, who, bringing several boats, immediately set about constructing a boat bridge. The professor ordered that they should be allowed to proceed; he had precise instructions from Monsieur Duvivier regarding the best mode of defense to employ in such circumstances. The bridge was therefore completed comfortably. The head of an attack column did not hesitate to rush onto it—but then Samanou sent an elephant forward over the plank of a see-saw. The weight of the beast immediately raised a large sluice gate; the level of the water dropped rapidly.

The scene that followed was horribly dramatic. As the waters flowed away, they uncovered monsters with viscous skins—and these were not made of wood. They were alligators and the long water snakes that earned Africa its ancient name of Ophiusa.[41] The hideous swarm became indescribable, and the denouement can

---

[41] In fact Ophiusa (Ophiuse in French), meaning "land of serpents" was a name given by the ancient Greeks to a region in Portugal.

easily be imagined. All the men at the head of the column were stifled by the coils of the snakes or chopped into pieces by the jaws of the saurians.

"Well," said the pitiless Isidore, "what do they have to complain about? Those who were working this morning had dolphin and salmon for breakfast, and those that built the bridge just now were served fish even stronger than the allibamba of the Congo. Oh, what fish! To think that today is April the first![42] If Monsieur le Professeur would like lunch, Monsieur le Professeur is served!"

On Monsieur Cornelius' instructions, Samanou closed the sluice gate that had been opened; then, with the aid of his elephant, he operated another sluice gate. More water flowed in and covered the theater of the frightful carnage—a theater that Isidore deigned to find admirably designed—with their broth.

The following day, April the second, a further attack was launched, but in a different direction. The Galla had discovered a section of wall in a poor state, almost in ruins, and, in consequence, amenable to scaling. The ditch that opened in front of the wall was free and uninhabited; it even seemed to have been long abandoned, for tufts of grass and brushwood could be seen growing in it. The besiegers risked themselves at that point. Having crossed the palisade and the stockade, a few men descended into the ditch.

Professor Cornelius, who had been give orders by the Commandant, told Popo to hold his fire. The employment of the batteries might have intimidated the assailants, and it was necessary, on the contrary, to inspire a certain confidence in them. The head of the column

---

[42] In France traditional April Fool's Day jokes are known colloquially as "poissons" [fish].

descended, and then the whole assault column massed in the ditch. At the foot of the rampart, as at the top, there was a profound silence. The climb was about to commence.

Then Samanou, at a sign from Cornelius, had the elephant concierge open a door giving access to the ditch, but cleverly hidden from enemy eyes by leafy bushes.

Immediately, a legion of elegantly formed animals flowed into the ditch, panting and making prodigious leaps.

"What are those creatures?" asked Isidore, who was still keeping close company with the professor. "They're not lions like the ones that attacked me, and they're not panthers. One might think that they're dogs."

"Yes, yes—they are dogs."

"Well, my compliments to the Messieurs. They're leaping at our enemies' throats in fine style, bleeding them like pullets!"

"They are, indeed, stranglers, who do their work, as you can see, silently."

"That's true. They're taking hold of their prey without uttering a syllable. The inhabitants of this city are very clever to have had the idea of forming a brigade of dogs of that size."

"Oh, the idea isn't new. The majority of ancient peoples had dogs of war. The mastiff teams of the Cimbrians, Gauls and Spaniards have their page in military history, but combat packs were employed most frequently in antiquity by Africans, who were named Cynamynes for that reason."

The work of death was completed. All the Galla that had taken part in the expedition were lying on the ground, their throats torn open.

Then the mossenga Samanou imitated the cry of a toucan. The dogs went back to their kennels; the elephant closed the door again.

"It's funny, all the same," said Isidore to Professor Cornelius, "that the dogs don't bark. How do they do that?"

"Pliny says that the ancients took away the voices of their mastiffs by making them swallow a frog."

"That's just like us, then. You can be sure that the jokers who eat frogs don't talk about it."

Chapter XVII
Entrance on Stage of the First Actors
in a Combat Menagerie

The fact of those two successive checks inevitably gave the Galla food for thought. Their ardor appeared to have cooled somewhat; the days of the third, fourth and fifth of April passed without notable incident.

Monsieur Duvivier took advantage of that respite to hasten the execution of his projects. Everything was going as desired, but he was, he said, only half way through the task as of yet. Monsieur Fresnel, constantly on the dock, only went away from time to time to go up to the observatory and scan the horizon.

The Galla were holding still in their lines.

Professor Cornelius was permanently on watch on the ramparts. Isidore no longer left him. Samanou and Popo were only waiting for his orders. Everyone was ready, beasts and men alike.

On the seventh of April the defense had a sharp alert, and the professor took the opportunity to note that the number seven is fateful among the Galla.

On the seventh, therefore, the besiegers made a further attempt on the terrain where the first column had tangled with the teeth of the mastiffs. They arrived in enormous numbers. When they were in the ditch, Samanou had his elephant open the door to the kennels.

It is well known that there are more than a million dogs in France, eighty thousand of them in Paris alone. If Professor Cornelius had been able to summon to the rescue a good contingent selected from the elite of the

Parisian pack, he might perhaps have been able to ward off the effects of an assault, but the canine troop of Kisimbasimba counted scarcely a hundred heads. The brave four-footed companions ran at the enemy, leapt at throats and ripped bellies, but they could only make inroads into the lateral surface of the compact column, so tightly grouped were the ranks—a true ant hive. In spite of a few bites, the column got through; the scaling of the ruined section of the wall was attempted, and the escalade was a complete success.

The Galla were on the terrace of the rampart!

Monsieur Cornelius and is men had prudently beaten a retreat behind the ivory palisade. The sun was setting. The Galla made camp where they were, not daring as yet to advance across the booby-traps of the esplanade.

During the night of the seventh and eighth of April, Monsieur Duvivier deployed various transparent phantasmagorias, one of which represented two goats slain by a lion—but the arguments emitted by the courbache were doubtless more conclusive than the inspirations of holy terror, for on the morning of the eighth, the attack columns had the audacity to rush forward again. The men comprising them were pricked by the caltrops, entangled by the networks of hippopotamus hide thongs or fell into the leopard holes, but in the end, the column passed. As it moved forward, it destroyed the accessory defenses.

Commandant Fresnel, hastening to the location, immediately had a few ballista shots fired, but the rain of projectiles had no effect on the compact masses, which were growing incessantly. It was necessary to use the lithoboles. Enormous blocks of stone fell upon the Galla. Wasted effort! Even the largest missiles hurled at the human avalanche caused no more damage than revolver bullets fired into a swarm of locusts. The assailants kept coming.

What were they to do?

On the order of the Commandant, Samanou went to fetch six enormous black lions from one of the city's ditches: the most terrible animals there are in the world once they are under the spur of terror themselves.

The wild beasts were brought to the palisade. There Samanou guided them into a cage, stimulate them and then, opening a door to the esplanade, launched them all forward at once.

The stimulation was not obtained this time by means of an ablation of the caudal appendage; the mossenga had quite simply imitated the crow of a cock-erel. The lions, gripped by fear, had set off like arrows.

The big cats precipitated themselves in two bounds upon the assailants, disemboweling the first ones who fell under their claws, but it was impossible for them to open a breach in the ranks of the multitude. They disap-peared, strangled and swallowed up by the heaving mass.

"Come on, Samanou," said Commandant Fresnel, "we don't have a moment to lose; it's necessary to charge, and charge full tilt!"

The mossenga was ready.

Calm and sure of himself, like a trainer in the an-cient Roman circus, he had to hand a company of shock troops, and was only waiting for a signal from the mas-ter.

At that signal, he opened a large barrier, given free rein to eight rhinoceroses, previously driven into a fury. Foaming at the mouth, their eyes ablaze, the large pach-yderms charged head down at the rabble of Galla, and made deep holes therein. Scarcely had it opened up, however, than the human tide closed up around them.

Nevertheless, a certain disorder had been imported into the bosom of that ocean of black heads; an initial quake had been produced; the astonished avalanche came to a halt.

In order to emphasize the effect that he had just sketched out, the worthy Samanou hastened to let out a troop of twenty buffaloes excited by intoxicating beverages. Recklessly, the buffaloes charged, stabbing the disunited Galla with their horns and goring a considerable number, thus bringing about the commencement of a disintegration.

The moment was decisive; it was necessary to take advantage of the opportunity.

For that purpose, Samanou had kept in reserve a herd of wild boar, exasperated in accordance with his savant principles. That was a method known to Maréchal Bugeaud,[43] well enough that he had been able to apply it successfully to enrage dromedaries on the day of the battle of Isly. The mossenga had coated the boars with a layer of tar, and then set fire to them!

The herd thus launched charged at great speed, striking the assailants with blow after blow of their tusks, and succeeded in breaking the formation.

Complete disarray!

The Galla, losing all appetite for their fruitless attack, beat a retreat in the direction of their bivouacs.

The besieged breathed deeply.

---

[43] Thomas Bugeaud (1784-1849) was the Governor-General of Algeria when the Battle of Isly was fought on the Moroccan border in 1844.

The day was not yet finished, however. An hour after the check, the enemy had reformed, and attempted an offensive return. The troops—fresh troops—emerged on to the esplanade with a brigade of sixteen elephants forming the head of the column.

Insensible to the rain of projectiles that arrived upon them from the batteries of lithoboles, the huge animal engines advanced as far as the palisade. They were demolition elephants, marvelously trained. Having quickly understood what their drivers were demanding of them, each of them attacked a paling, shook it, pulled it up and eventually uprooted it—and then attacked another.

It was easy to see that a breach—a wide breach—was about to open up. A few more seconds, and the last retrenchment of the defenses could not fail to be broken down. Behind the elephants the rabble of Galla was howling with all the force of their lungs the *barrit*, the ancient war cry of the Roman legionaries, ready to attempt a supreme effort.

That was what the defenders could hear and see; they thought they were doomed.

It was then that an idea of genius traversed the brain of Professor Cornelius.

What an inspiration it is! He has glimpsed a means of salvation.

The scientist whispers a few words in Samanou's ear. The mossenga runs to the animal pens and comes back carrying a peccary in his arms.[44] Then, without

---

[44] The term "peccary," like the previously employed terms "alligator" and "jaguar," is nowadays used specifically in application of American animals, but terminology was much looser in the 1880s and the Spanish *pecari*, to which I have

wasting a second, he attaches the peccary to the palisade and suspends it there by its tail.

Surprised by the pain, the peccary utters piercing screeches. Its desperation increasing, it strings together ear-splitting roulades.

The elephants stop, dazed and consternated. Then, they promptly turn around.

Gripped by panic, crazed with terror, they stampede, bowling over, trampling underfoot and crushing everything in their path. They break through the infantry that they were serving as a covering mass, for whose action they were preparing the way.

This time, it is not a retreat but a veritable rout of the aggressors. Their defeat is consummate. They turn on their heels and retrace the route to Kifoukourou in total disorder.

---

supplied the English derivative, would have been used to refer to any kind of small pig.

Chapter XVII
The Fantastic Tortoise

The besiegers had been rudely repelled.

Feeling that they had experienced ill luck thus far, they seemed to submit to a temporary depression, and remained immobile in their lines during the ninth and tenth of April. The defenders took advantage of that respite to repair the palisades, block the breaches and reorganize the accessory defenses.

In the harbor, Monsieur Duvivier's workshops did not pause; the engineer was only asking for another four or five days of toil. At all costs, it was necessary to hold out for another four or five days.

Commandant Fresnel had high hopes of succeeding in that. However, it was always necessary to be wary of the Galla. Their last misadventure had doubtless surprised them, but not discouraged them. They did not lift the siege.

It seemed just to conclude from that fact that they were meditating a new attack, planning some calculated operation. In any case, it was necessary to be on guard. Monsieur Fresnel clung more assiduously than ever to his observatory, interrogating the enemy front with circular scans.

On the evening of the tenth of April, his telescope, aimed in the direction of Kifoukourou, presented him with the image of a gray object whose form was difficult to determine. One might have thought that it was a huge tortoise asleep on the sand. Darkness was falling. It was impossible to carry out more ample observations, from which some clue might be obtained as to the nature of the strange object.

The following day, the eleventh, the Commandant was at his post at first light. The tortoise, as he called it, had not changed its position, but it seemed to be larger than the day before.

It was a gray mass veined with white, which was swelling up by the hour. By midday, it was enormous. Its carapace was patched with violet-tinted scales.

What was that extraordinary animal, that monster whose apparition carried the mind back into the night of time, and made one think instinctively of paleontological creations?

The observer lost himself in conjectures. Profoundly astonished, he could find no plausible explanation for the phenomenon.

The tortoise with the changing hues was now growing visibly.

Finally, no longer able to contain himself, the Commandant had the engineer Duvivier and Professor Cornelius climb up to the observatory in order to obtain their opinions.

Each of them, one after the other, put his eye to the telescope, examined the object patiently and minutely, and...did not know what to say. The fantastic animal varied its colors like a chameleon, and was still growing. The tortoise was now the size of a small hill.

"I've got it!" exclaimed Cornelius, all of a sudden. "I think I know what it is. The besiegers are changing tactics. Now they're working after the fashion of moles."

"What do you mean?"

"That the Galla have just opened a mine shaft—that they intend to get in here by a subterranean route. That hill you can see growing and taking on various tints is the rubble, the accumulation of earth that our enemies are in the process of extracting from the subsoil."

"You think so?"

"I'm sure of it. Here, look carefully. You can see spadefuls of white clay or red sandstone being thrown up onto the heap."

"What! It's hardly likely that these barbarians have had the idea of such an enormous project! It's implausible."

"No, not in the least. Mining is a well-known mode of attack. All the peoples of antiquity employed it. It's a primitive method, which corresponds to the infancy of the poliorcetic art. Don't be astonished by the fact that the Galla know how to construct subterranean tunnels."

"What are you saying?"

"The truth. Do you want to make sure? Order a reconnaissance. If you wish, I'll send Samanou this evening. He'll be able to tell us what's happening in the enemy camp, and perhaps even take prisoners to obtain any information we might lack."

"All right—let him go take a look, and bring me back a Galla."

At nightfall, the brave mossenga departed, and once outside the fortress began to creep silently toward the point designated by the name of "the tortoise." He had donned two disguises, cleverly superimposed: immediately over the body, an antelope skin, after the fashion of Makololo spies; on top of that, a tiger skin, after the fashion of the negroes of Benguela. Thus adorned, he could inspire terror or covetousness at will.

Half way between the fort and the camp at Kifoukourou he lied down on the ground and put his ear to it. He could distinctly perceive the sound of tools. The enemy was definitely building a tunnel, and deploying a singular activity in that work. The professor was not mistaken. To convince himself further, the mossenga thought that he ought to press on to the heap of rubble. There he saw laborers at work. No doubt was any longer possible; the Galla were taking the subterranean route.

His mission completed, the explorer was getting ready to return to his departure point when he was suddenly surprised by a chorus of cries of fright. He had been seen!

Frightened by the sight of a tiger, which reminded them of the recent exploits of the animals recruited by the defense, the Galla infantrymen fled in disarray. Their clamors did not disconcert Samanou. He threw himself into a little ravine, left the carnivore's skin there, and continued his route costumed as an antelope.

As it happened, in spite of his extraordinary precautions, he nearly ran into a sentinel. The latter saw him. He stopped, tranquilly, and pretended to be grazing, without taking his eyes off the enemy. The sentry, putting his weapon on the ground, advanced slowly and stealthily, in order to grab hold of the prey....

At the right moment, Samanou seized him around the legs, threw him to the ground and briskly tied him up and gagged him. Then, loading him onto his shoulders, he returned to the fortress with his prisoner. The imprudent sentinel would furnish complementary information regarding the situation of the besieging army and the intentions of the Mata Sonapanga.

Commandant Fresnel knew, therefore, that the tunnel was well-advanced, and that by that means the enemy was counting on emerging promptly into a natural tunnel passing under the fort—a tunnel whose existence was revealed to them by old traditions. He leaned that the Galla warriors were being encouraged on the warpath by all manner of methods. They had, for instance, recently been given an ointment that would render them invulnerable—a philter prepared by the Tringlote, with the blood of a newborn child. The oracles had been consulted; a cockerel, immersed in water several times, had not drowned; a pullet had drunk the celebrated *benghi* poison without dying. Everything seemed, therefore, to presage victory.

Unfortunately for them, the Galla saw one shadow in that cheerful picture. The country that they had ravaged so thoroughly could no longer nourish them; their provisions of food were exhausted; there was famine in the camp. Already, the men were no longer eating anything but grass, leaves, mushrooms, bats, earwigs and pigeon guano, of which they had discovered a deposit. A meager pittance! Even those eccentric foodstuffs would soon run out; then, following the orders of their military authorities, the Galla would officially turn cannibal. To maintain that army of five hundred thousand men, it had been decided that the gangas would kill a few hundred every day.

A situation like that could not reasonably be prolonged. In consequence, the Mata Sonapanga wanted to finish it very quickly, at any price. It was absolutely necessary for him to take Kisimbasimba, which he knew to be rich in provisions of every sort.

Such was the information that the defenders extracted from the Galla prisoner. Commandant Fresnel was justly worried. Was it not to be feared that the enemy would soon discover the natural tunnel the prisoner had mentioned? If what the man said was true, ought they not to expect at any minute to see a troop of assailants emerging inside the fortress, charged with clearing a passage for the rest of the diabolical army? How could they defend themselves? How could such a catastrophe be prevented?

They spend the days of the twelfth and thirteenth of April in mortal anxiety.

The Commandant had no other preoccupation than that of stimulating the constructions demanded of Monsieur Duvivier, no other desire than seeing their imminent completion realized. Everything was, at any rate, going well in the workshops of the harbor. The engineer only needed another two or three days of work.

"As long as the enemy leaves them to us, those three indispensable days! If we have our freedom of movement during that short space of time, salvation is not impossible!"

Such were the hopes to which the defenders were clinging.

On the fourteenth, the Commandant gathered the members of his general staff together at lunch. The table was set up under a sycamore, not far from the threshold of the hut with the conical roof that had received the affectation of the general headquarters.

A hundred paces from the flagstaff where the French colors were displayed, the steps of a ruined temple rose up. It was a monument in the Egyptian style, the construction of which Professor Cornelius had attributed to the time of Ptolemy Philadelphia.

Isidore was serving.

Suddenly, the attention of the guests was attracted by an unusual sound coming from the direction of the ruins, ordinarily silent and deserted. One might have taken it for the blows of a sledgehammer trapped beneath the staircase.

They listen carefully. No, it is not a mistake. It really is the repeated impact of some heavy instrument analogous to a sledgehammer. At intervals, the noise stops. The blows can no longer be heard—but then it is another tool that is employed in attacking the edifice. The steps shake; a hidden hand is disturbing their arrangement, putting weight on the stones in order to dislocate them.

There is no doubt about it; it is the attacking miner, who has succeeded in discovering the famous tunnel. He has followed that subterranean communication; at any moment, he is going to emerge into the fortress.

One of those psychological moments is nigh, which bite and tear the best tempered of hearts.

"Messieurs," says Commandant Fresnel, simply, "it's not possible to beat a retreat. You're not yet ready, are you, Duvivier? No? Well, all we can do is sell our lives dearly."

The Commandant picks up his rifle, and waits.

The steps of the stairway oscillate, dislocate and are lifted up. A large collapse occurs, and the ruins disappear momentarily, drowned by a flood of dust.

As the cloud dissipates, a human form appears.

Yes, it is a man: a man dressed in the manner of the assailants. It is the first miner emerging.

"Keep calm!" says Monsieur Fresnel. "Aim carefully. Fire one after another. The first Galla's mine!"

He raises his rifle—but Isidore stops him, shouting: "Commandant, without commanding you, don't shoot! Don't you recognize him? That fellow is Chocolat!"

Chapter XIX
The Mysterious Quarter of the Enchanted City

It was, indeed, Chocolat.

Everyone recognized him now, and could not help bursting out laughing. It really was him, still as tall, still as thin and as gracefully emaciated as before. He was wearing the costume of a Galla captain that Isidore had made him put on in the times of his grandeur. He still had his provision-bag slung over his shoulder—the famous bag that was rendering clinking sounds.

They hastened to surround the mulatto and question him, but the tall fellow scarcely made any reply except for brief invocations of San José de Cacuaco. Then, overwhelmed by emotion, combined with the pleasure of his reentry to the fold, he said, in a cavernous voice: "I'm hungry. Señor Isidore, *da nobis*, something to eat!"

On the Commandant's orders he was immediately awarded everything there was on the table. The excellent Chocolat did not need to be invited twice. He went into action vigorously. In a matter of minutes, all the remains of the feasts had disappeared, including the guests' unfinished portions.

"Well, you haven't changed," said Isidore. "Still the same, indefatigable for substantial dishes. Come on, you're better now, aren't you? Tell us how you were able to rejoin us. Where the devil have you come from?"

"He can tell us while we walk," the Commandant interjected, "because we must, without losing a minute, retrace his steps with him—that's of the utmost importance. The communication that our mulatto has just opened up might be nothing other than the mysterious tunnel we've been talking about—the natural gallery into which the enemy miner is trying to break. That's what we need to ascertain as soon as possible."

A quarter of an hour later the Commandant penetrated beneath the parvis of the Egyptian temple in the company of Professor Cornelius. Isidore marched ahead of them with Samanou and a few Biribis carrying tools and torches. Chocolat served as guide to the little column.

The explorers traversed marvelous catacombs, a high gallery with an arched vault—or, rather, a series of immense hemispherical grottos linked by narrow passages opening in their piedroits at ground level. Similar to cathedrals, these grottos had been formed by nature, but the alleyways that connected them bore traces on their sidewalls of work accomplished by trenchant tools. Elsewhere, human hands had left their undeniable imprint everywhere. Gigantic statues were carved into the granite of the catacombs; bas-reliefs appeared similar to those found in Nubia, but more primitive in style. Professor Cornelius stopped several times to consider a panel, probably symbolic, representing a seated man with a war drum to his left, with a lion showing its tongue, a goat and a dog at his feet. Pebbles scintillated on the floor of the grottos, the gleam of which was marvelous. The professor picked up a few of them; they were gold nuggets.

"Let's go," said Commandant Fresnel. "Let's make a quick reconnaissance of this chaplet of crypts. It's important to check as soon as possible what the Galla prisoner said, to which our mulatto's subterranean journey adds, you'll agree, some probability. But I can see other corridors to the right and left the branch from the direction we're following. Is our guide sure that he's not mistaken in guiding us along the route he took through this maze? Ask the man, Isidore."

"Let's see," said the cook. "Have you got the thread of the thing, as the great writer said whose name I no longer know and you don't either. Do you recognize these caves?"

"Yes, Señor Isidore, me *recognosco* myself perfectly."

"You're lucky. How the devil do you do it?"

Triumphantly, Chocolat showed the kitchen-master the reference markers that he had strewn along the route, in the manner of Petit Poucet. They were swallows' nests that he had detached as he went along. He had devoured a considerable number, but, with the prudence of a hungry serpent, he had spread even more on the ground, in order to assure himself the subsistence throughout the return journey, if he were forced to retrace his steps. That was superb: he had not made any mistake!

They marched in that fashion for more than two hours. They estimated that they had covered three or four kilometers underground when they reached an opening through which daylight was coming.

"*Hic*, Señor Isidore," said Chocolat, firmly. "*Hic cecidi* in the hole."

They were on the edge of a ditch open to the sky.

The cook-ganga-ya-ita's former kitchen orderly then unfurled in sober terms, decorated with Latinisms, the story of his odyssey, from the night when he had escaped from the camp at Kifoukourou.

The first steps he had taken, by a fortunate hazard, had brought the fugitive to the baggage hut. There, groping his way, he had filled his supply bag with tins of food. Following the principle of mariners, who never embark without biscuit, he did not want to set out en route without solid provisions of campaign food. And those supplies had constituted a reserve only to be touched in case of absolute necessity.

Thus resupplied, he had succeeded in avoiding the vigilance of the sentinels; he had run at random, and run and run…so hard that he had fallen into a ditch covered with branches, doubtless an elephant trap. He had spent the night there and, in the morning, had set out tranquilly through this gallery, the entrance of which he had eventually found hidden behind some brushwood. His subterranean voyage had been accomplished without hindrance—a real pleasure trip. The tunnel had been illuminated in places by natural fissures filtering the sun's rays gently, well ventilated by chimneys, well watered by limpid streams and plastered with delicious swallows' nests. Plenty to eat and drink: a veritable paradise!

He had strolled, and marched, on and on…until he had found the end of the tunnel. There he had seen light through the obstacle that formed the end of the tunnel and made it a dead end. Daylight was filtering through cracks in an old wall. He had struck a few blows with a stone to enlarge the cracks, to see whether he could get through to the other side of the wall. His curiosity had nearly cost him dear, since his measured blows had provoked a rock fall, from which he had miraculously emerged safe and sound, thanks to the intervention of San José de Cacuaco.

While Chocolat told his story, Commandant Fresnel had examined the vicinity of the ditch and directed his telescope at the surrounding area in all directions. He saw that the exit opened on the far side of the camp at Kifoukourou; that the hole served as the external orifice of the catacombs; that the gallery revealed by Chocolat's itinerary could be considered as a long postern of the besieged fort, and that if they had been numerous it would have been possible to carry out a fortunate sortie by that route to attach the Galla from behind. But what could forty-seven men do against such considerable forces? Evidently, it was necessary not to think of a solution of that nature. Better to continue with the plan they had traced out.

Having made that sage resolution, the Commandant immediately had the bay that led to the ditch blocked up; then he gave the signal to return.

As they traveled through the magnificent catacombs of Kisimbasimba in the inverse direction, he verified the assumption that the sequence of vaulted crypts connected by corridors pierced in the piedroits constituted a main artery from which a number of other galleries branched at intervals. Having taken the precaution of bringing his pocket compass, he was able to penetrate into some of those immense lateral caverns. The first he visited was grandiose in its proportions. The vaults fashioned by Mother Nature were supported by colonnades, primitive in style but majestic, showing signs of the work of the human hand. Analogous to the grottos of Makanna, which open on the banks of the Loufira, were those substructures not ancient temples?

Another lateral gallery was remarkable by the fact of its freshness and the sounds that were escaping from it. There were violent murmurs, growls and rumbles similar to those of distant thunder, but continuous and more strident. A very simple examination permitted the explorers to take account of the causes of the phenomenon. The tunnel in which they found themselves was fashioned similar to the system of caves of Makouammba, which also open over the Loufira, in that the extrados of its ceiling served as the bed of a stream. One could distinguish in the tumult the roulade performed by the fast-flowing waters from the dull sound originating from a waterfall.

A third gallery was equally noisy. In that one it was the river itself that was flowing openly beneath the higher vault. The waters of that underground gulf were as black as those of Erebus. There was nothing astonishing in that, but other phenomena threw the voyagers into profound surprise. An unexpected spectacle: the watercourse was carrying myriads of sparks! Like the Phlegeton of the mythological Hell, it was flowing in places in flames.

Frightened, the explorers retraced their steps.

The next tunnel was more hospitable. It was a branch, vaulted with a neat arch, the section of which testified to the exclusive work of human hands. At the extremity of the subterranean vault a few rays of sunlight peeped through. They went on to the end. There, Professor Cornelius uttered and exclamation equivalent to Archimedes' *Eureka*. The tunnel opened into the ditches of the fort, into the menagerie of wild beasts. Another ramification of the same tunnel led via various meanders to each of the ditches of the lions of the interior.

It was by means of these hidden pathways that the animals received their food. Fresh footprints were visible in the soil.

Some of these grottos, therefore, were inhabited! One could assume that they served as subterranean dwellings for the inhabitants of the city, whose disappearance they had not understood. They were in the presence of a semi-troglodytic population!

Everything was explained.

Isidore, however, could not explain everything about Chocolat's odyssey. While they went back to the city, and the Commandant was engaged in animated conversation with Professor Cornelius, Isidore took the mulatto aside.

"You've told us how you fell into the hole and subsequently got into the tunnels; that I understand. But how the devil did you get out of your sack? How were you able to undo the stitches?"

Chocolat smiled. He had not undone the stitches of the antelope hide sack; he had eaten his way out!

Chapter XX
Tenebrous Machinations

On his return to the general headquarters of Kisimbasimba, Commandant Fresnel imparted his perplexities to his general staff. He had been struck by the military properties of the grottos he had just traversed. Those subterranean cavities, in fact, constituted a veritable redoubt in which it was permissible to seek refuge in case of a success by the besiegers. One could barricade oneself within them, defend them, and sustain a battle inch by inch. By concentrating a part of the vast provisions stored in the fort under its enormous cupolas and destroying the rest, one would only leave a supposedly triumphant enemy and empty city, deprived of means of subsistence, and, in consequence, untenable for an army as hungry as that of the Galla. Finally, the catacombs, opening to the country, offered a line of retreat that one could, as a last resort, attempt to take. Ought they to abandon, in favor of this new opportunity, projects on which they had been working for a long time and already nearing their conclusion—a conclusion that they hoped to be able to attain shortly?

There was considerable embarrassment.

Before making a decision, Commandant Fresnel went up to his observatory again. The extracted soil was still piling up at the entrance to the mines of attack. The original mass was scarcely growing any longer, but two other heaps, already considerable, were forming on the side of the first, in the direction of the enclosure, indicating the direction of the tunnel being dug.

The catacombs offered the defense a ready-made system of counter-mines. Was it not appropriate to march right away to meet the enemy miner? The Commandant thought so, and ordered a further exploration of the magnificent natural galleries in consequence. The previous day, wandering through them somewhat at hazard, they had cocked an attentive ear everywhere, and listened carefully, not without anxiety but fruitlessly. They had not perceived any sound revealing subterranean movements. This time, they knew the direction that the assailants were following, and with the aid of the compass, they ought to be able to catch them in the act.

On the fifteenth of April, therefore, they undertook a further visit. The little expeditionary column, formed as it had been the day before in terms of personnel, carried more complicated equipment and a larger provision of tools of every sort. On the other hand, following the prescriptions of Professor Cornelius, Samanou had charged the Biribis with a number of wooden crates of various shapes and sizes. Chocolat, marching at the head of the column, was carrying a large earthenware lamp at the end of his extended arm. With that primitive torch, the tall mulatto was reminiscent of a grotesque caryatid—one of those bronze torchbearers that light the courtyards of princely edifices.

They walked along the main artery. Every time they went past the opening of one of the branches extending from that major gallery, the Commandant interrogated his compass in order to determine the direction of the branch. Following the indications of the needle, he groped his way along the branch carefully. He set his ear against the lateral wall or the floor. Nothing. There was nothing to be heard. Professor Cornelius then set a pan full of water on the floor. The water at the liquid surface remained motionless. He placed light particles—grains of millet—on the surface of a kind of Basque drum. Not a single grain budged; the tambour maintained absolute silence.

Finally, after a considerable number of vain investigations, the millet jumped timidly, to the rhythm of a vaguely perceptible but significant noise. Everyone was able to observe it, irrefutably, in his turn: methodical work was being carried out underground. The direction of the ripples in the water in the pan soon indicated the direction. They were on the track.

As they went further in the right direction, the grains of millet jumped higher on the drum and the ripples in the liquid became little waves. Soon, the sound even became perceptible to the ear. The further they pushed forward, the more it gained in intensity. No error was possible. The particular sound obviously resulted from rapid blows struck upon rock, the execution of a miner's work. They were soon able to convince themselves that the miner was operating at a lower level than the tunnel they were in. After a little groping, they succeeded once again in determining in a precise manner the verticality of the head of the subterranean brigade. There, the grains of millet fell back in the precise point from which they had been projected into the air. The ripples in the liquid were circular and concentric with the rim of the drum.

"That's it," said Professor Cornelius. "Our assailants are two meters beneath our feet."

"Good," replied the Commandant. "We need to take them from behind. Let's operate a few meters behind the crew."

That was what they did. Professor Cornelius was equipped with a trepan that Monsieur Duvivier had ordered the blacksmith to make expressly for that purpose. The apparatus was operated by hand, like the capstan of a ship.

The rock only opposed slight resistance; it was a rather soft sandstone into which the bit entered without difficulty. The bit rotated silently. After seven or eight turns, the trepan was lifted up. A semi-cylindrical ladle then withdrew the rubble of the crumbled rock from the hole.

The operation required several hours. It was necessary to proceed without making a noise, in order not to disturb the Galla miners. It was even necessary to increase prudence as the thickness of the ceiling of the mine was felt diminishing under the bit.

Fortunately, the work was brought to a successful conclusion. Nothing remained at the bottom of the excavation but an extremely thin crust still separating the two camps. Professor Cornelius could hear the Galla talking. He then requested absolute silence, had a number of containers placed on the rim of the hole, told Samanou to hold himself ready and Chocolat to extinguish his lamp.

The enemy miners were singing as they worked. Isidore, always full of wit, observed in a whisper that they were singing "in a minor key."

Samanou then took a stick, and with a sharp blow punctured the crust of rock that was no more than a few millimeters thick. The enemy did not react to the fall; they continued their work. All was going smoothly.

The mossenga grasped a long conical container, took out the stopper and poured the contents into the excavation, which he immediately sealed with a plug. Then he waited, ears pricked.

After five minutes, a few exclamations of surprise were heard and a few cries of amazement.

The coup had succeeded!

Samanou put his hands on the other containers that were within reach, and extracted objects, whose forms the darkness prevented from being distinguished, but whose presence was manifested by a train of luminous dots, as shiny as carbuncles. Those objects slipped one by one through the excavation and fell into the assailants' mine. Samanou replaced the plug.

He listened....

This time, there were cries of pain and fear, then moans and howls of human voices. Then...nothing more. Everything fell silent again.

"Complete success!" said Professor Cornelius, in a low voice. "Let's obtain all the useful consequences from it. Now that our enemies are dislodged from their subterranean workshop, it's necessary that they don't come back any time soon."

At these words the mossenga took a soft body from another container, analogous in every respect to a snake, and passed it through the hole. The cylinder was long enough to descend to the floor of the Galas' mine while its other end still remained on the floor of the gallery they were in. Then the professor had the lamp lit again, set fire himself to the end of the serpentine form, and had the orifice of the excavations sealed with potter's clay.

"Now," he said, "you can be sure that they won't be back for some time—not before five or six days."

Commandant Fresnel was delighted. Five or six days! That was twice as long as Monsieur Duvivier needed to finish his work. Then they would have the right to count on the salvation of which they had despaired so many times. Fresnel, ordinarily so impassive and calm, did not hesitate to manifest a satisfaction to which the noisy joy of his little escort responded.

Even Chocolat, exultant without knowing why, brandished the staff from which his lamp was suspended like a drum major's baton. Suddenly, however, he dropped the lamp, exclaiming in bewilderment: "*San José de Cacuaco, ora pro nobis! Ora pro nobis, Cacuaco!*"

The lamp had gone out—but the catacombs had not returned to darkness.

On the contrary, they were illuminated in the manner of a cathedral choir on the evening of a festival.

A troop of armed men equipped with torches was heading straight for the little column.

Chapter XXI
England and France

"This time," said Isidore, "I believe our situation is clear. We're trapped. I recognize my diabolical army. While we thought we were smoking them in the Gallery of Panoramas, here they are, emerged from under the stage by another trap door. It's curious, if you like, but not funny."

The torch-lit troop stopped dead.

At the blast of a whistle, the men forming it took aim at Monsieur Fresnel and his companions.

The Frenchmen had been discovered.

There was a terrible moment of silence. They expected a general discharge.

No rifle shot was fired.

"Halt! Who goes there?" a clear voice was heard to cry, in English.

"What!" said Professor Cornelius. "They speak English, these Galla!"

"It's bizarre," replied the Commandant, "but it's a fact. Nothing as crushing as facts! Isidore, they're shouting '*Halte*' and '*Qui vive?*' at us in English. Reply loudly and firmly."

"France!" said the former zouave, in the tone that he had once adopted when responding to the entry on duty at the casbah in Medeah.

"Halt!" repeated the voice. "Advance one, and give the parole."

"They're asking for a negotiator. Go forward, Isidore."

The zouave, who did not understand anything of what was happening before his eyes, nevertheless hastened to step forward.

"Advance! Halt!" he heard again, when he was a few paces away from the enemy troop.

"All right, understood," replied Isidore. "We're halting." He stopped, put his heels together, struck the pose of an unarmed soldier very correctly, and...what a surprise! The people who had hailed him were not Galla. The troop they had encountered underground did not belong to the diabolical army.

A man detached himself from the group and approached Isidore. The man was white, of the European type. The small flag he was holding bore the English colors.

The two negotiators looked at one another in amazement, and two exclamations were emitted in unison.

"Oho!"

"That's a good one!"

The Europeans who met one another thus in the catacombs, several thousand leagues from Europe, had a momentary desire to embrace one another, but their emotion was containable. The man with the flag contented himself with handing his interlocutor a card.

"To the French gentleman," he said, in English. "Go swiftly."

"I don't understand," Isidore replied, "but I know what you mean. It's necessary to take this to the boss. On my way."

And, arriving back at his own people, he added: "This is getting stronger and stronger, Commandant. It's not the diabolical army. Here, this is what he gave me for you."

Commandant Fresnel took the slightly dog-eared card, lit his pocket torch and was able to read:

Capt. HARRY FOX
H.M. 2nd Foot
Quartered in the East India 2nd Madras Infantry
Traveler
From SOUAKINE to LOANDA via TANGANYIKA

"Well," said the Commandant, "if it hasn't been given to us to meet Lovett Cameron or Henry Stanley, there's still Harry Fox!"

In pencil, he wrote in his pocket book:

Hippolyte FRESNEL
Frigate Captain
Voyager
From Loanda to Souakine
Via Tanganyika

He tore out the page and handed it to Isidore.

"Go," he said. "Take that to the English voyager."

"English! Impossible! Me, I'd have bet on the Prussians. But the English—bravo! They're on our side."

Isidore hastened to carry out his master's commission, and the man with the flag transmitted the sheet of paper to a person who had emerged from the gloom a few paces behind.

Then strident blasts of a whistle were heard, and shouts of: "Hurrah for France! Hurrah for France!"—to which the Frenchmen hastened to reply: "*Vive l'Angleterre!*"

With that, Chocolat who had fallen face down on his lamp, got up again briskly. San José de Cacuaco was decidedly a great help to him, since he had just changed Galla into Englishmen. The jack-jack knew the English well. He had seen many of them in Saint Paul, where they carried out all the major commerce. He had even served aboard their steamers, which operated the Kwanza service under the Portuguese flag.

"*Viva la reina! Viva la reina Victoria!*" he shouted, at the top of his voice. "*Bravo Cacuaco! De gratias!*"

Commandant Fresnel and Captain Fox had gone to meet one another. They saluted each other, and then shook hands cordially.

Harry Fox was a man of about thirty, of an uncommon height and vigor; he could have served as a model for an artist who had dreamed of creating a type of Anglo-Saxon Hercules. A long blond beard prevented the analysis of his facial features; one could only discover their veiled and impenetrable blue eyes, imprinted with the stamp of a singular energy, and thin lips, parted by an ironic and semi-icy smile.

After a few minutes of expansion, he said: "May I be permitted to ask Your Honor what he is doing under these vaults, where I was about to fire at you?"

"That's precisely the question that I was going to ask Your Honor."

"My presence in this pace is easily explained. I was making a patrol in the dependencies of a State placed under the protectorate of the queen of England."

"Personally, I was defending a territory that I'd deem myself glad no longer to have to cover with my protectorate, I can assure you."

And the frigate captain gave the English voyager an abridged account of his expedition across Africa.

"We've been tracing the same itinerary," said Harry Fox. "We're marching in the opposite direction; we were bound to encounter one another. As for me, this is my story:

"I'm involved at this moment in a bet of twenty-five thousand pounds sterling, almost the total value of an inheritance I'm due to collect. When I talked about taking the *via Tanganyika*, people laughed in my face and thought I was mad. Why, I ask Your Honor? What's so ridiculous about taking a route that will soon be as banal as Park Lane or your Avenue des Champs-Élysées? Via Tanganyika is a geographical expression that has nothing extraordinary about it today, when opinion is sending Europe forth on the conquest of the African continent, creating companies like your Association des Deux-Mondes for the development of civilization and the extinction of the slave trade in Africa, when governments are only thinking about the railways to be built here—when, for example, the Portuguese parliament has voted forty millions to the effect of linking their colonies in Mozambique to that of the Congo. But you know all that as well as I do, and better. I'll get back to my story.

"I came through the valley of the Nile. The functionaries of His Highness the Viceroy of Egypt gave me a frosty welcome almost everywhere, in spite of the elevation of the temperature, and even though I was carrying an order of service from the queen's government. I was also equipped with a host of letters of recommendation, and a wad of firmans of every species. Those papers didn't do me much good on Egyptian territory, and I firmly believed that beyond Fakoda they wouldn't do me any good at all. I was mistaken, as you'll see.

"From Fakoda I went up the Nile Valley as far as Ismaila—which some pronounce Gondokoro. I visited Kamrasi. In passing, I went to ask King Mtesa for lunch, whose address I had because Speke and Stanley had been to see him before me. Mtesa hasn't yet understood the elegant mechanism of constitutional government. He treats his subjects a little like domestic animals, and his cuisine is detestable. I taught him to drink champagne. He's a faithful friend of England.

"From there I came down to the Victoria-Nyanza, which I traversed like Stanley, and here I am on the Tanganyika."

"Good—but I don't see what use the firmans you mentioned just now were."

"I'm getting to that. When I arrived in this region I was admitted to the court of the Sultana Touloumia, the sovereign of Mkinyaga. I gave the queen the letter of service from my government, secured by a large seal of red wax. She took the seal for an image of the sun and treated me quite simply as a Loumotto—which is to say, a son of the sky—and lavished me with her good graces. She smoked my pipe, and I smoked hers. We made the exchange of blood, from which it followed that I got Touloumia to consent to a good treaty of offensive and defensive alliance with Great Britain. You can see that my letter of service had some utility."

"And how, finally, did you arrive in these catacombs?"

"You'll see. The Estates of Queen Touloumia extend far beyond the north of the lake. Her capital, Akribanza, is more than sixty miles from here. It's a city in ruins. I've seen cisterns there of a very remarkable architecture. The construction of those edifices is attributed by the indigenes to a very ancient race of white men. For the Arabs of the vicinity, of course, it's the work of Solomon, the son of David, who, as everyone knows, had genies to undertake his public works. I spent several fortnights in the royal palace of Akribanza. Her Majesty Touloumia is proud to bear several sonorous titles signifying that her sovereignty is considerably absolute. A host of domesticated lions that circulate freely in the apartments of that Queen of Sheba are the living symbols of her incomparable power. However, Touloumia was notified of the formation in the east of a swarm of locusts with human faces."

"Ah! Now we're getting there!"

"Yes, soon. It's necessary to tell you that Mkinyaga is a true kingdom of Amazons. Touloumia dresses as a man and also makes the Princesses Halimah, Zenza, Oulimenga and Foume-a-Kenna—charming young women who already smoke a pipe like a midshipman— wear masculine costumes, too. The personnel of the queen's army are entirely feminine and armed with long-shafted lances. When I say that *all* the troops are formed by individuals of the weaker sex, that's not quite accurate; the queen has a bodyguard composed of fifty men, and those men are dressed as women. There's doubtless some traditional artistic reason; presumably, the inventor of the etiquette in question wanted to produce an effect of contrast. At any rate, the imminence of an invasion of barbarians frightened the populations of Mkinyaga greatly. Queen Touloumia summoned me to produce the first effects of the treaty of alliance contracted between her and the Queen of the United Kingdom. There was no hesitation; I immediately put the bodyguard on a war footing; I gave them all my trading rifles. I also had a few barrels of powder. Then, to manufacture cartridges, I was obliged to use my papers, the letters of recommendation with which my portfolio was bulging. You can see that my firmans have been good for something."

"Very interesting. Go on."

"The barbarian advance guard pushed on as far as Akribanza. The court thought it ought to emigrate and take refuge in its summer palace, a country house maintained in case of invasion."

"So the queen is here, somewhere in these grottos?"

"Of course. Can you imagine that these eastern barbarians, these invaders of Queen Touloumia's kingdom, have contacted me and offered me—would you believe it—the rank of generalissimo of their armies?"

"Of ganga-ya-ita?"

"Exactly."

"It's a position that one of my men has recently occupied...a trifle reluctantly, I ought to say."

"Like it or not, that man was able to take service with the Galla. He was only responsible to himself for his actions, but I wasn't free. I had engaged and compromised my government with regard to a queen—a queen of savages, but still a queen. My duty was, therefore, to remain faithful to her. That's what I've done. I followed the court and took refuge with her in these subterrains."

"May I ask what you did to get in here? We've never been able, in spite of our investigations, to discover how or by what route the population of this strange city disappeared. I've told you that while we were beating a retreat before the Galla, we found ourselves mixed up with these brave people. We ran with them into the stronghold. Then, when the first excitement was past, we wanted to get to know our saviors, to see those who had given us shelter. But they'd vanished!"

"And me, too. I'll show you which way we went. Please follow me. Don't worry about going astray; I'm admirably familiar with these secret places, where I'm in command—for I'm in command of the queen's forces here: the fifty bodyguards, to whom I've returned the clothing of their sex, and which I've reinforced with the men of my escort. That little troop is placed under the orders of my manservant, Jackson, who served as my negotiator just now. Although singularly restricted in numbers, these forces suffice for me to maintain my role.

"My mission is simple. While the waves of the barbarian invasion batter the foot of your walls, I remain sheltered in these vaults, as if under an umbrella when it rains. I wait here tranquilly for better times. I shall only emerge when the storm has passed. Between now and then, what do I have to do? Very little. Supervise the maintenance of the royal menageries; have food distributed daily to all the animals defending the borders of the subterranean palace; guard these surrounding galleries that serve as exterior boulevards to the habitations of my troglodytes, while watching over the exists to the surrounding countryside; and especially, to forbid any human being access to the subterranean road—the one we're on, which puts the grottos in communication with the interior of the fort."

The voyagers had arrived at the extremity of a tunnel ending in a somber black gulf exhaling thick vapors. Harry Fox sent a few men on ahead, who held their torches high.

A steep staircase connected the tunnel and the gulf lost in the shadows.

"If you'd care to go down," said Harry Fox, "I'll show you the route that we followed."

Chapter XXII
The Phlegeton

Before setting foot on the first step, the faithful ally of Touloumia sent away his troop of bodyguards, with orders to return to the palace of the troglodyte queen; he only kept for an escort his manservant Jackson, armed with a torch and still carrying his flagstaff bearing the English colors. In the same way, Commandant Fresnel invited Cornelius to go back to the city via the hole in the temple stairway, and to take Isidore, Samanou and the Biribis with him. Following the example of the English gentleman, he was only accompanied by one man, charged with the task of lighting the way with a resin torch. The man to whom this mission of confidence was entrusted was, as you will have deduced, Chocolat.

Preceded by their torchbearers, the two voyagers went down.

At the bottom of the staircase, which had no less than a hundred steps, a polished, shiny surface appeared, extending into the dense darkness. It was that of a subterranean river, whose velvety waters, as black as those of the Styx, reflected the light of the torches garishly. A little inlet opened at the foot of the stairway, and a canoe was moored in the inlet.

"Let's get aboard," said Fox. "We have to go downriver now; it joins the river that gives access to the fort. You're an officer in the French navy; do me the honor of taking command of my vessel."

Fresnel saluted the English gentleman.

The four men took their places in the boat. Chocolat held the two torches, one in each hand. Jackson sat at the rear, where the English colors floated, and took charge of the tiller. They moved rapidly, following the flow of the water. Flocks of nocturnal birds wheeled slowly around the flamboyant torches.

In the course of that sinister navigation, Commandant Fresnel observed to port considerable numbers of long boats moored side by side along the bank, some of which were laden with logs and others with planks.

"Those," said Fox, "are the constitutive elements of the pontoon bridge that, by putting the harbor of the city in communication with the catacombs, permitted us to effect our movement. When the retreat was complete, the bridge was packed up and stored away here, where you can see its materials."

"That's why we couldn't understand how the population had disappeared. The sudden eclipse seemed inconceivable to us."

"You can see that the means were well planned, prepared far in advance and well hidden after the operation."

In the meantime, they had arrived at the confluence. The subterranean river that they were following emerged into a broad watercourse, similarly subterranean and somber.

It was necessary to take the thalweg of the river.

"A little to starboard!" ordered Commandant Fresnel. When the maneuver had been carried out, he said: "That's it!" in his firmest voice.

They were heading toward the harbor. Large birds, abruptly awakened, were coming to brush the fuliginous flames of the torches.

"Oh!" cried the Englishman, suddenly. "What's that upstream?"

"Fire," the Commandant replied.

"Oh! Where is it coming from?"

"I don't know, but we're probably engaged in the river that we recognized higher up during our exploration of the grottos, in the course of which flames were flowing, and which we baptized the Phlegethon."

"But how do you explain the origin of those flames?"

"I don't explain, my dear Captain, I merely observe. We're downriver of the blaze."

In fact, the upper reaches of the river no longer presented anything to the eye but a vast scene of conflagration. The banks, the waters and the vault all seemed to be prey to the conflagration.

"It really is the Phlegeton," repeated the Commandant. "The peril is serious. There's only one thing we can do: run. It's necessary for us to flee before that firestorm. Get going—and may God protect us!"

"All right!" replied Fox.

The two voyagers took an oar each, and began to row.

The flames followed them. Fiery globes detached from the blazing mass seemed to be about to bite into the stern of their boat; they could already feel the radiant heat…another cable, and the conflagration would reach them. The navigators of the new Phlegeton were going to perish miserably, burned to a crisp and reduced to ashes.

Chocolat and Jackson had thrown away their torches, unnecessary henceforth. They relieved their masters and made vigorous efforts in their turn…but the blaze, still gaining, threatened to surround the craft. It was necessary at all costs to prevent that from happening. They therefore made for one of the sidewalls of the Phlegeton in order to let the incandescent mass pass by. Fortunately, the navigators were able to moor in a little cavity forming a creek.

Huddled in that hole, shielding their faces with their hands in order not to be blinded, they glimpsed the great floating fire, which seemed to have been vomited by the Inferno, pass before their eyes. It was a raft laden with combustible materials, which were crackling and spitting in every direction. The heat that it was giving off was very intense, further increased by virtue of the reflection of the calorific rays from the stalactites and the rock; the facets of the vault sent back that intensity no less vigorously. The tunnel's network of ledges and soffits functioned like the reflector of an enormous rotisserie. A moment came when the voyagers were able to believe that they were being roasted alive, but it was only a momentary alarm.

The pyrophoric raft had gone past.

It was necessary to hurry, however: to descend as soon as possible in the wake of the monster, because another fire was visible upstream. It was necessary to take advantage of the brief interval during which navigation was free.

The boat emerged from the creek, therefore, and, like the boat of the ferryman Charon, hurtled into the darkness, allowing itself to be carried by the current. The darkness did not envelop the travelers for long, however. Already, solar light was reaching them from the mouth of the tunnel.

With a few strokes of the oars, they arrived in the harbor.

There, however, other dangers awaited them. Their craft emerged into a semicircle of pirogues stationed in ambush. The crews of the pirogues were formed by negroes armed with hooks, gaffs and long pikes, similar to the halberds or hanicroches of the Renaissance period.

The poor people who have just escaped the flames of the Phlegeton as if by a miracle will not escape death this time: a frightful death, that of Captain Cook in the Sandwich Islands! They are about to fall under the blades of savages!

The savages, however, stand still, as if petrified, their arms raised and their gaffs poised. They dare not hook the boat or strike those manning it. More than that, they utter cries of surprise and joy. They are not enemies, then. No, they are Kabindards, some fifteen of the brave workers employed by the engineer Duvivier. Monsieur Duvivier himself is standing on the dock of the harbor.

He extends his hand to the voyagers.

"You've run great dangers," he says. "It'll soon be twenty-four hours straight that the Galla has sent us fireships. They're the masters of the upper reaches of the subterranean river. Our secret is no longer unknown to the enemy. How and by whom was our plan revealed to them? Probably the prisoner that Samanou took, who disappeared two days ago. I suppose that he escaped via the lake. What's certain is that the assailants have tightened their blockade in that direction. The Galla want to burn our *Saint Michel*.

"What's a *Saint Michel*?" asked Captain Fox.

"The vessel we've just constructed in order to break the blockade. We baptized it thus in the hope that it might permit us to reckon with these demons and pierce the lines of the diabolical army."

"Oh! It's a monitor—a blockade-runner."

"Yes," said Fresnel, "A blockade-runner. Would you care to come aboard—we'll examine its organs and you can give me your opinion." The Commandant continued: "As you can see, it's a battleship whose original design does the greatest honor to our engineer, Monsieur Duvivier."

"Yes indeed!"

"It's a daou with neither masts nor sails, as flat as a pontoon, but the deck is protected by a roof.

"Yes, like the celebrated *Atlanta*, the ironclad used by the Confederates during the Secession."

"That's right. Except that, for want of iron, we've made all our armor-plating from the hides of rhinoceroses, elephants and hippopotamuses."

"Well done! As soon as I get back to London I'll publish that ingenious idea in the great industrial journals, *Iron, The Broad Arrow* and *Engineering*—with your permission."

"Go ahead. You see those two wheels arranged symmetrically on the flanks of the vessel? That's the system that will serve for our propulsion. Except that, for want of a steam engine, we have a carousel turned by two pairs of buffaloes."

"Very good! As soon as I get back to England I'll inform the *Mechanic's Magazine* about it, if you approve."

"Gladly. Now, as you can imagine, we have neither cannon nor powder, so our armament is formed by neuroballistic artillery. Look, here are two eight-caliber lithoboles—which is to say that they can launch eight kilogram stones—and onagers that project bombs, by which I mean earthenware vases full of disagreeable materials. We also have 'dolphins'—they consist of an apparatus in the form of a gallows designed to drop heavy perforating or contusive bodies."

"Perfect! As soon as I set foot in Liverpool, I'll send a special article to the *Naval and Military Gazette*, if you have no objection."

"None. You can also inform the editor of the periodical that our blockade-runner has a spur at the prow formed by four elephant tusks solidly bound together and fretted."

"Good—very good, perfectly good! Very ingenious!"

"You're too kind."

"No! But in your place, I'd have set aside all these little tricks. You'll never piece the lines of these barbarian sailors with that, Monsieur. Their flotillas of pirogues are as dense and compact as shoals of herring."

"That's your opinion?"

"Yes. You'd do better to destroy this little naval construction, this delightful bootjack...."

"Bah!"

"...Burn the entire stock of your provisions...."

"Damn!"

"...And take refuge with me in the grottos."

"Really! But tell me, my dear Captain—why didn't you propose that to me the other day, when we came into the city with the queen and her people, and with you?"

"Why didn't I take you in via the boat bridge on the Phlegeton? My God, it's quite simple—you hadn't been introduced to me."

"Ah!"

"But today it's quite different. I know who you are: a brave French officer full of energy. You've visited me in the catacombs, where I command in the queen's name. I can receive you."

"Thank you!"

"Commandant," Monsieur Duvivier interrupted then, "We'd do well to accept that offer. We probably won't succeed in forcing the blockade—and then, at any moment, in spite of the devotion of my Kabindards, an enemy fireship might make contact with our *Saint Michel*...and all would be lost. These incendiary devices are arriving without interruption, almost regularly, every ten minutes. There are all sorts of things on those burning floaters: fatty substances of every sort: oil, grease, human cadavers, bundles of ivory and empty crates. I've found some that belonged to us. I even recognized in that fashion a few objects with no value in the eyes of the Galla, but enjoying, in their view, one essential property: combustibility. Fortunately for us, not all of these floating pyres are equally well lit; some of them go out *en route*, or burn poorly, or don't burn at all. Look— there's another of these infernal machines arriving that isn't on fire."

The mouth of the Phlegeton gave passage at that moment to a floating body of rather strange form. It was a little *tinghi-tinghi*, or natural raft, covered with a cradle of lianas. The engineer had the apparatus hooked with a gaff, stopped within the blink of an eye, and inspected.

Beneath the primitive canopy a human body was in repose, extended like that of the infant Moses on the day when he was saved from the waters by the Pharaoh's daughter. It was not a corpse but a body full of life. Who was the man, then, and what had he come to do? Was he a spy, a lost child or a fanatic sent by the Mata Sonapanga to destroy the blockade-runner and cut off the Frenchmen's retreat, at the cost of his life?

The man seemed to be sleeping peacefully. His visage was placid, his complexion florid, his plumpness enormous."

"That's a fat body," said Captain Fox.

"San José!" cried Chocolat. "*Gloria tibi*, San José, you who have saved us!"

The tall mulatto had recognized the man. It was Mimoun!

Chapter XXIII
Chocolat's Tins

Abruptly torn from his drowsy state by the rude hands of the carpenter who had just cut the lianas of the raft with his hatchet, the worthy Mimoun began by putting his hand on his heart and murmuring: "Allahu Akbar!"—God is great.

Then, recognizing those who were surrounding him, he said to them, one after another: "Greetings, Commandant! Hello, Monsieur Duvivier! How are you, Chocolat?"

Having said that, the excellent Mimoun told the story of his life, from the famous day when he had been put in the sack. The heroic-burlesque odyssey was sung by the hero himself, in the delightful hybrid idiom known as the sabir tongue.

This, in brief, was what had happened to him:

Imprisoned in his animal skin, where he was waiting resignedly for the moment to render his last sigh, the spahi had suddenly felt himself lifted up, loaded onto the back of a man and carried away hastily in an unknown direction. He told himself that his hour was nigh, that he was being taken to the Tarpeian rock from the height of which, under the terms of his condemnation, he would be hurled into the lake, and that, since it was written that he must die in that fashion, there was nothing to be done but to praise God, repeating endlessly: *Alhamdulillah!*"

After a certain time in transit, however, the combination of the porter and his living burden had suffered a violent shock. The animate vehicle had come to a halt;

Mimoun felt himself laid on the ground. Then, obliging hands had opened his sack, and he found himself face to face with a woman with robust shoulders, a powerful neck and arms muscled like those of an athlete. The woman, a harpy, was laughing in a strange fashion. By that laughter, modulated in a minor key, the spahi had recognized the sorceress who had previously made so many grimaces at him—the one that General Isidore had called the Tringlote.

Well, he said to himself, very calmly, *it's doubtless written that I'm not to be drowned in the waters of the Tanganyika. My terrestrial lot is to perish at the hands of a foreign woman. Thus will I perish, then, if it pleases God.*

Contrary to his funereal presentiments, Mimoun-ben-Abdallah had not been put to death by the Tringlote. The latter had, on the contrary, shown herself to be full of attentions for him. Enclosed in a hut isolated from the camp, the prisoner had been marvelously cared for, nourished and pampered. His diet, however, had been singularly monotonous. He had been nourished entirely on milk. Even so, the quality of it was agreeably varied; sometimes it was goat's milk or ewe's milk, sometimes the milk of a bitch or a she-monkey.

On that regime the spahi had put on weight, and the sorceress rejoiced in seeing the flourishing condition of her protégé. In a period when famine was rife in the camp, where anthropophagy had become routine in the army of Gallas, the worthy woman had feared for the life of the man she had saved from the waters of the lake. She had made great efforts to hide him from all eyes, principally those of the sacrificers. Having found a place propitious to her designs on the bank of a river, she had constructed a very solid *tinghi* there, with a roof of lianas. She had put Mimoun in that nest, skillfully hidden in the reeds, recommending to him silence and immobility. The prisoner had had no cause to complain. Within that cradle clad in foliage he slept at his ease and drank milk.

Such was Mimoun's story.

He did not know any more and wondered how it had had been given to him to find himself in the midst of his own people like this. It was explained to him that the Galla, considering the use that might be made of a *tinghi* containing a large and fat fellow, had probably intended it to play the part of a fireship. Mimoun admitted the likelihood of the observation, which seemed all the more plausible to him because he had seen himself briefly surrounded by flames and that he remembered his *tinghi* smelling of burning.

Chocolat remained intrigued, however. He wondered why the Tringlote had thought she ought to appropriate Mimoun and feed him on a diet of milk. To fatten him up, undoubtedly, but why cause that? Among the Galla, the reply was made to him, obesity doubtless constituted an item of physical beauty, as in all the lands of the Orient. Evidently, the sorceress, smitten with her captive, intended to ask for his hand.

That explanation, however, only partly satisfied the mulatto. He therefore imparted his personal impressions to his old companion in misfortune, prudently following them with a question mark.

"So," he said to him, "the Galla señora had resolved to marry you? You were to contract *matrimonium*?"

"No," Mimoun replied, modestly, once he had understood the question. "No, Madame Tringlote did not want to marry me."

"Well, *quid* then?"

"She was going to eat me on the first day of the festival, the day when the city was taken."

The following day, the seventeenth of April, Captain Harry Fox was preparing to return to the catacombs—not via the Phlegeton, of course, but through the gap in the staircase of the temple. Before leaving, he had a serious conversation with Commandant Fresnel.

"You've mounted a fine defense," he said. "So long as you were able to put up a reasonable resistance, I carefully refrained from treading on your toes. The French colors were flying over the city; I didn't want to detract from their glory. But today, you're convinced, as I am, that all resistance has become impossible. You're at the end of your resources and strength. In three days, or two, or perhaps tomorrow, the five hundred thousand invaders surrounding you will reckon with your forty-seven men. You can't think of sustaining this titanic struggle.

"On the other hand, I repeat to you—and you share my opinion—that your blockade-runner will have great difficulty emerging safe and sound from the ordeal to which you want to submit her. Well, once again, renounce the struggle. Destroy everything, materiel and provisions. Bring your flag with you and come with me to ask Queen Touloumia—the ally of my own gracious sovereign—for shelter. There you'll be out of danger. There, under the English flag, we'll only have to remain still and wait patiently for the storm to pass.

"When the barbarian hordes have disappeared over the horizon, we'll emerge from the grottos, and we'll head for Saint Paul together, via Tanganyika—for I won't forget my bet. Make up your mind."

Commandant Fresnel had moist eyes. Silently, he extended his hand to the English gentleman. The sacrifice was consummated; he confessed himself beaten.

Before retreating into the catacombs it was indispensable to give orders.

The engineer Duvivier, consulted by the leader of the expedition, declared that the blockade-runner would be completely organized within thirty-six hours, armed and ready to emerge; that the ship having now become unnecessary, it would scarcely take an hour to reduce to nothing the work that had taken so many days of hard labor; and that, to sink the little boat, it would be sufficient to open the panels in the ballast-hold and pierce a few holes in the hull below the flotation line.

"Do it," said Monsieur Fresnel.

The engineer immediately headed for the harbor.

The Commandant had also sent for Monsieur Cornelius; he wanted to give him the responsibility of disarming the ramparts, destroying the neuroballistic artillery and of setting fire to the food stores.

The professor did not appear. The Commandant was told that he had returned to the catacombs, where he was listening, in the company of Samanou, because it seemed to him that the enemy had resumed the labor of mining.

At that moment, Isidore ran up, out of breath.

"I've come from the ramparts," he said. "Monsieur Cornelius left me on sentry duty there... Oh!"

"Well?" demanded the Commandant.

"Spit it out, then," added Captain Fox.

"Well, Messieurs, it's unfortunate, but the Galla are in the city!"

"In the city!"

"Yes, a bad business! They launched an attack. I fired at them, with the Bibiris, but they ended up breaking through. They've all hastened in their wake. Their Mata Sonapanga is at the head of the column. They're coming—they're close behind...and look, here they are!"

The diabolical army had, in fact, finally contrived to force a way through the outer walls. A famished host was swarming into the fort, uttering cries of ferocious joy as if in chorus.

"Not a moment to lose," said Captain Fox. "We have to get back to the grottos."

"Impossible!" replied Fresnel. "That human avalanche is blocking the way. We're already cut off from the temple staircase!"

"Yes," Isidore affirmed. "They've already reached Chocolat's hole."

"We're doomed, my dear Captain, and it's me...."

"Doomed! Why? It's sufficient for us to beat a retreat. Let's fall back to the harbor, embark, and break through the blockade."

"The *Saint Michel*! But you said yourself that she's an impotent and ridiculous blockade-runner."

"Too bad—but we don't have any alternative, and for want of anything better...."

"You're forgetting that I've given the order to sink her."

"Damn it! That's serious!"

"Run, Isidore—countermand the order. Stop Monsieur Duvivier!"

The cook set off like an arrow.

The Galla were still advancing.

The Biribis having rallied, Fresnel ordered them to begin precision fire. The circumstances demanded that

203

this time, the powder must speak, even though they had very few cartridges. Captain Fox and his manservant, Jackson, each armed with a sixteen-shot rifle, supported Fresnel bravely, firing at the attackers.

Every bullet felled a Galla. Alas, that was an insignificant result. What could a few rifle shots do against such a compact mass? Was it possible for a handful of men to hold countless hordes at bay for long?

"Without wishing to command you, Commandant, hold on, hold firm—the *Saint Michel* is as solid as the Pont Neuf. Everything's ready on board; we can set sail whenever you wish."

It was Isidore who spoke thus. He was at the head of ten Kabindards, armed, like him, with carbines.

"Good," said Fresnel. "Now there's hope. We can beat a retreat coolly and methodically."

"Hang on, old fellow," muttered the former zouave, who had started shooting in his turn. "Just wait there— I'll settle your hash. *Bang!* I believe that's it. It seems to me that I got my man!"

Immediately, there is tumult in the Galla ranks.

Their columns stop. Circular eddies are produced in their mass. What is happening?

As you will have guessed, the former laureate of the firing range, the drummer Isidore, has hit the Sonapanga.

They take advantage of that moment of confusion. They retreat to the port, while firing at the enemy. They reach the dock! Quickly, they embark. They prepare to cast off.

"Let's see," says Monsieur Fresnel. "General staff, Biribis, Kabindards, is everyone here? Is everyone at his post? Make a roll call. With Captain Harry Fox and Jackson, Chocolat and Mimoun, whom we've recovered, there should be fifty of us on board, all told. Count well!"

"No," said Isidore, "not everyone's here. Samanou hasn't replied *present*, nor has Monsieur Cornelius. They're still out there, you know, in the tunnels you call catacombs, like those under Montrouge, not far from the Gare des Sceaux."

"My God!" What can we do?"

"Poor Samanou!"

"Let's go find them."

"No, it's impossible."

"Poor Monsieur Cornelius!"

While these dolorous exclamations are overlapping aboard the *Saint Michel*, immense clamors rose up, which bring forth violent echoes from the city. They are no longer, as there were a little while before, cries of war or triumph. It is a concert of moans, screeches and terrible howls, a mixture of plaints that seem to voice rage, terror and despair.

"In the name of Heaven, what's happening?" the passengers on the blockade-runner ask one another, tremulously. "Alas, there's no doubt about it—our companions have just fallen into enemy hands. They're being massacred and we can't help them. Oh, unfortunate Samanou! Poor Monsieur Cornelius!"

Commandant Fresnel has reflected. The situation is grave, the moment decisive. It is impossible to go ashore to attempt to prevent a disaster. It is impossible to remain moored in the presence of the victorious Galla. Those tenacious warriors will not be shaken for long. They will resume their forward movement. In ten minutes they will be on the quays. There is only one way out of the predicament: it is necessary to leave, as quickly as possible.

The previous day, Monsieur Duvivier has had the bottom of the piles of the barricade sawn through. Those piles are now only maintained in place by a few strips of wood. A hawser is attached to it, and the Kabindards haul away. The boom collapses. The entrance to the harbor is clear. The pass is free.

En route!

The *Saint Michel* moves off and leaves the harbor. She is on the waters of the lake!

It is just in time, because the horde of Galla has erupted onto the quays—but those victors are flooding onto them in extreme disorder. They are raising their arms to the heavens as they run. They seem bewildered. Their cries and howls have redoubled their intensity.

The passengers cannot comprehend such disorientation on the part of the new masters of the city, but they do not have the leisure to seek an explanation. There, on the lake, are other adversaries, to whom they must face up resolutely. No hesitation! Clear the decks for combat and forward ho!

The *Saint Michel* performs well. With the first thrust of her spur she has broken through the blockade-line of the besiegers. She is out of the prison! Unfortunately, the impact has reduced her speed. The enemy craft are gaining on her; she might not get much further.

Alas no—now she is surrounded!

Daous, rafts, dugout canoes—a thousand vessels of every species—have surged forth from all points of the compass and formed a circle around their living prey. Other boats are still appearing. They are flying over the lake and thickening that iron band. The blue waters of the Tanganyika can no longer be seen. Its surface has disappeared beneath a forest of floating wood.

The *Saint Michel* defends herself! Her dolphins drop enormous bocks of stone, sinking the pirogues that dare to draw alongside her. Her onagers hurl a hail of earthenware pots onto the decks of the enemy daous, inside which are balls of venomous serpents whose bite is fatal, as immediately fatal as that of the speckled cobra. The fall shatters the vases, and the fearful crewmen scatter or jump into the water. The crenellations of the blockade-runner give passage to the barrels of rifles, and every rifle shot fells an attacker.

Alas, the Galla have a vast numerical advantage. Scarcely has one of their vessels sunk when it is replaced by ten more. When one of their sailors is hit by a bullet, fifty new assailants are there, advancing the position that the victim occupied.

On board, three Biribis and as many Kabinards are already out of action. To complete the misfortune, Monsieur Fresnel has been hit in the chest by an arrow. Fortunately, the wound is not serious, but it is painful, and it causes him to suspend the exercise of his command.

The Galla are getting bolder. Now they are diving into the water like the Malays of the Indian Sea, in order to attempt to board the little battleship. Around the sides, the stern and the bow of the ship, multitudes of black heads with flat hair appear, like bouquets of aquatic plants with grimacing faces. Some of those intrepid individuals climb up, catch hold of the rigging and leap onto the roof that protects the deck.

The defenders of the *Saint Michel* have not ceased fire. They are still shooting…but alas, it is their last bullets that they are firing. Captain Harry Fox has emptied his cartridge case. One more rifle shot and then…nothing more!

The English gentleman fires the final cartridge. That done, he bends down tranquilly over Monsieur Frennel, who is lying on a reed mat.

"It's over, Commandant," he says to him. "I've lost my bet. I shan't arrive in London via Tanganyika. It's a pity to remain half way. We have no more to do than save honor and respectability. We can't decently fall into the hands of these freshwater mariners. What if we were to blow ourselves up?"

"Blow up!" replied Monsieur Fresnel, with a bitter laugh. "We don't possess a grain of powder."

"Well, that's true. Then I propose the damp path instead of the dry one. What if we were to sink ourselves?"

"You're a worthy officer, a brave man. Take command of the ship and act as you see fit."

"Yes sir, directly!"

"Your hand—I'll shake it one last time."

"Certainly! Gladly...."

"Forgive me! It's because of us, and for us, that you're here, that you're going to die! If you hadn't encountered us, you'd now be sheltered in the grottos."

"Oh well! I would have liked to win my twenty-five thousand pound bet, but I accepted my loss ten minutes ago. It's all the same to me to be aboard your little ship. I told you that it wouldn't get through—but that's not the question. The essential thing is to know that she can't be running any danger, and I know that she isn't."

"Who's *she*?"

"Queen Touloumia, the faithful ally of Her Majesty the Queen of Great Britain. God save the Queen! I can assure that it's all the same to me, provided that we die an honorable death, Monsieur Duvivier can sink us quickly. England forever!"

"Listen—I can only do one last thing for you that will give you pleasure, but I offer it to you."

"What's that?"

"At the moment when we moved off, I had my colors nailed to the stern of the *Saint Michel*, just in case. Nail your flag alongside my tricolor. Our national colors will disappear together beneath the waters of the lake, while we die as brothers."

Captain Harry Fox was unable to open his mouth. The humorist was profoundly moved. He clasped the hand that the wounded man held out to him, and disappeared.

A witness to that heart-rending scene, the excellent Chocolat felt overwhelmed by an entirely legitimate emotion. So, even though he had eaten breakfast at dawn, and very solidly, as was his habit, he experienced at that moment a sharp need for refreshment.

Alas, he, too, observes a heart-breaking fact. It is not only cartridges that were lacking aboard the *Saint Michel*. His private provisions of food are also exhausted. He has nothing left in his sack but six cans of preserves. When he has consumed the contents, the game bag with the joyful metallic clink will no longer ring with anything but emptiness, or rather nothingness. A sad—a very sad—prospect!

However, the lanky fellow plunges his hand into his sack in a melancholy fashion and pulls out a can—a tin-plated cylinder of respectable diameter. It is doubtless marinated tuna....

He will soon find out, because Chocolat took out his big knife. He gets ready to prize open the lid, with a dexterity born of long practice.

At that moment Isidore arrives, who has also come to visit his master—a final visit! He perceives Chocolat, who has completed his operation. He sees what the tin contains.

His arms fall inert by his sides, so great is his shock—but the prostration does not last long.

"Monsieur Duvivier!" he shouts. "Monsieur Duvivier! Stop again! Don't sink the ship! Monsieur Fox—where's Monsieur Fox? I need to talk to Monsieur Fox!"

The English captain is unable to reply. He has just been struck by a hatchet at the moment when he was setting up the two flags side by side at the stern of the blockade-runner. He has lost consciousness, and blood is inundating his face.

"Monsieur Duvivier!" Isidore repeats. "Monsieur Duvivier, look at these—look at Chocolat's tins!"

Having verified the exactitude of what Isidore has observed, the engineer immediately summons the carpenter and the mechanics. The latter hasten to bring long spars of wood, to the end of which they attach the tin-plate cylinders.

"All done?" says the engineer. "A bit of fuse, now—fix it! Everything ready? Right—light up!"

The fuses are set alight, and the spars thrown into the water to either side of the *Saint Michel*, level with the quarters.

Scarcely ten seconds have gone by when two mighty explosions are produced, almost simultaneously, one to port and the other to starboard.

In making his last provisions Chocolat has made a mistake. What he had mistaken for tins of food, for a meal, were dynamite cartridges.

Chapter XXIV
Deliverance

The explosion of the makeshift torpedoes improvised by Monsieur Duvivier was followed, a few moments later, by considerable effects. The passengers aboard the *Saint Michel* saw four enemy daous plunged under water, twenty pirogues hurled into the air, a dozen rafts blasted to smithereens and the debris of all those vessels raining down into the lake, pell-mell with dead or wounded men.

All the Galla swimmers were struck dead; their bodies were floating in the midst of a hecatomb of fish and hippopotamuses, similarly thunderstruck.

An admirable spectacle for the Europeans who were about to perish—a terrifying one for the savages who thought they had won!

The flotilla of the Galla flees in fear.

The lake is free. They can continue out into open water—but no; one of the ship's paddle wheels has broken during that minute-long battle. The explosion of the starboard torpedo has smashed the paddles of the wheel. It is impossible to progress. The *Saint Michel* is wounded; she is condemned temporarily to immobility.

Thanks to the efforts of the gaff and the oar, the engineer Duvivier brings her to the shore of a little islet. There, delivered from her assailants, the blockade-runner can be repaired.

After a week, the desired repairs had been completed; the carpenter, the smith and the mechanics had caused that last traces of the damage sustained in the course of the naval battle of April the seventeenth to disappear.

While those tasks were being carried out, Dr. Quentin had lavished all his care on the wounded. Monsieur Fresnel was already much better; on the twenty-fifth, the doctor gave him permission to get up. As for Captain Harry Fox, his wound was serious. Nevertheless, all hope was not lost; they thought that they would be able to save him.

On the following day, the twenty-sixth of April, the Saint Michel quit the chance mooring and drew away from the shore of the island that had sheltered her. It had set a course for Kisimbasimba. It was a mission of discovery, to search for the absentees, Professor Cornelius and the mossenga Samanou.

The lake was deserted: not a sail on the horizon, not a single daou, canoe or raft. The flotilla of the diabolical army had left no trace of its passage over Lake Tanganyika.

They draw near to Kisimbasimba. No one! They cannot see anyone at all. It is deserted, abandoned, the extraordinary city where, a few days before, the land forces of the diabolical army were swarming, shouting and howling.

Everywhere, a deathly silence reigns.

Commandant Fresnel is notified of that fact. Equipped with his telescope, he gets ready to come up on deck. He is stopped on the way by a hand that is held out to him. It is the hand of Captain Fox.

"Monsieur," says the wounded man, in a faint voice, "I sense that I only have a few moments left. Listen to a dying man, I beg you."

"We'll save you."

"No, it's over, I assure you. I'm going contentedly, if you don't mind."

"We want you to live."

"No, no, I tell you. Listen to me. It depends on you whether I win my bet. In order to win it, I have to return to England via Tanganyika."

"Yes, we'll take you back by that route."

"Forgive me, Monsieur, I'm going to die—but it hasn't been stipulated that I have to come back alive. I can arrive back in London dead or alive, as I choose. Promise me that you'll take my body back."

The Commandant shakes the poor fellow's hand.

"Good," said Captain Fox. "Thank you. My bet is therefore won, thanks to your kindness. Twenty-five thousand pounds to come from my inheritance and the twenty-five thousand stake that's due to me—that makes fifty thousand pounds, doesn't it?"

"Yes."

"Please have the fifty thousand pounds given on my behalf to the director of the African Civilization Society. That makes, doesn't it, more than a million francs?"

"Certainly."

"I desire that that sum be employed to establish on a secure foundation, worthy of a civilized nation, the throne of Touloumia, the ally of Her Majesty the Queen of England."

"Very well."

"Now I can die in peace. God save the Queen!"

The Commandant is still holding the hand of the wounded man. That hand goes cold. The face is crimson. The doctor is called to the dying man.

Having arrived on deck, where he sets about commanding the maneuver necessary to pass through the mouth of the harbor, Monsieur Fresnel is surprised by an outburst of shouting—cries of joy!"

The passengers on the *Saint Michel* see the boat bridge emerging under the porch of the Phlegeton fill up with an immense crowd. They are not Galla! It is a part of the population in the midst of whom they found refuge on the thirtieth of January, and which then disappeared into the catacombs. From where have those worthy people reappeared, and what has happened in the strange banza? They will soon find out, for everyone can already see Monsieur Cornelius and Samanou standing on the harbor dock.

They have not been massacred, thank God! They have remained in safety in the catacombs.

Before going ashore, Monsieur Fresnel goes back to see the sick man. Alas, the Englishman is delirious. His words are incoherent.

"Salt!" he murmurs. "Very dear, salt! Imported from Zanzibar…negro money! Livingstone embalmed in salt….Livingstone to Westminster! Very rich, Harry Fox! Via Tanganyika!"

Emerging from the cabin, Monsieur Fresnel had difficulty holding back his tears

Having set foot on the dock, he fell into the arms of Monsieur Cornelius. The latter explained the events that had taken place in the city since the day he left.

With a skillfully aimed rifle shot, Isidore had wounded the Sonapanga. That had caused the initial flutter in the ranks of the Galla.

Taking advantage of that momentary disturbance, the worthy Samanou, who had just rallied the queen's bodyguard, demanded their collaboration in simultaneously opening all the ditches containing the lions.

Scarcely had the gates of the menagerie opened when between three and four hundred wild beasts had launched themselves on the shaken assailants—hence the cries of fright and the howls heard by the passengers of the *Saint Michel*.

One lion had hurled itself on the Sonapanga, who was already lying on the ground, and had killed him. Having lost their leader, the enemy fell into disarray. There was an immense, unspeakable, indescribable stampede.

The diabolical army had struck the camp at Kifoukourou, the camp and Nyonngo and all the other surrounding camps. Terrified, the barbarians had fled in an easterly direction.

Then, Touloumia had come out of the catacombs. Monsieur Cornelius had seen her and talked to her.

All kinds of peril having been averted, the queen of Mikinyaga had wanted to return immediately to her capital Aktibanza. She had departed the day before with her bodyguards and the princesses Halima, Zenza, Oulimanga and Foume-a-Kenna.

The entire court was laughing and dancing.

"One remarkable thing," said Monsieur Cornelius, pompously, "was quite astonishing! There were several hundred lions wandering in the city. Their work of carnage accomplished, although sated, they still had a menacing appearance. What could be done with so many inconvenient Bohemians? Samanou tried hard to get them to go back into their ditches, to master them by imitating all the tones of the cock's crow, but the beasts stayed where they were. They positioned themselves everywhere, in all the corners, licking themselves tranquilly, immobile on the stones that served them as pedestals, like the statues of lions, wild beasts of granite.

"Well, the queen only had to show herself, and all those beasts came to her like domestic cats, arching their backs and purring. Then, at a simple sign from her royal hand, those ferocious animals went peacefully back to their ditches, where the inhabitants of the city have continued to feed them. It's a menagerie unique of its kind! The docility of these domesticated lions is, I can assure you, incredible in its effects. It's the last word in the art of animal taming."

The hour of deliverance had sounded for everyone.

Isidore came in his turn to give Monsieur Cornelius the homage of his respectful felicitations.

"Let's go have lunch!" the professor replied. "There's no restaurant in the catacombs. For more than a week I've been eating nothing but swallows' nests and...."

"Monsieur is right—that's not very substantial...."

While serving the professor an exceedingly fine lunch, the cook, faithful to his old habits, engaged him in conversation on various topics.

"Explain to me," he said, "what you did in the catacombs to reckon with the diabolical army's miners. I don't quite understand what you did then with Samanou."

"Something quite simple. The first time, the mossenga threw into the hole a nest full of slightly drowsy wasps. The warm atmosphere of the mine woke them up abruptly."

"Oh, I understand that—I was the one who provided them."

"The second time, Samanou delicately introduced into the company of the unsuspecting enemy a band of lynxes, leopard-cats and other hungry carnivores."

"And the miners were bloodied like wood rabbits by a ferret! That's perfect."

"Finally, the third time, you saw me deliver the camouflet, and I did so in the ancient manner."

"As in the Middle Ages."

"And even before. The employment of that procedure is mentioned in history nearly two hundred years before our era. I therefore took a sleeve of cloth of a diameter equal to that of the hole. The cylinder was filled with toucan feathers and ibis down. I set fire to it; I blocked the holed and the tunnel filled with smoke."

"Some tobacco!"

"The smoke of those burning feathers put the mine tunnel out of action for some considerable time."

"Well, Monsieur, you win the plume! How does Monsieur find that elephant's foot and bananas?"

"Excellent!"

"And the zebra cutlet *au vin de palme*?"

"Delicious!"

"Well, I don't mind telling you, Monsieur, that there's still something that I haven't yet grasped."

"What's that?"

"You know the day when the Galla sent elephants to demolish our palisades?"

"Well?"

"Well, how is it that we got out of the affair when Samanou made his Saint Anthony's bird sing?"

"Quite simple again. I was lucky enough to remember that, among the terrestrial *fauna*, there are species separated by profound and almost insensate antipathies—that there are animals that horrify others. Thus, lions are frightened by the crowing of a cock; bears flee before horses; horses can't stand the scent of a camel or an elephant. The elephant itself is afraid of the cries of a pig. You saw that as soon as our peccary started making music, our assailants decamped."

"Brave little pig! By the way, Monsieur, is it true that the poor Sonapanga is dead?"

"Oh yes—he died under the lion's teeth."

"You know that he was like a Maréchal de France in the diabolical army. I knew him well, having been his deputy. Furthermore, he was the chief of all the magicians and other high priests of the god Ouaka."

"Ah!"

"He was, therefore, a holy Mata."

"Oh."

"And today, Monsieur…."

"What

"He's a *Mata mort*!"[45]

"Isidore, you're right. Your lunch was perfect, and you always have plenty of wit."

---

[45] This is a weak pun, *Mata mort* [dead Mata] being phonetically identical to *matamore*, itself a joke derivative of matador, referring to a slayer of Moors rather than bulls, or a braggart who represents himself, with a great deal of exaggeration, as a great warrior.

Epilogue

Before leaving the Enchanted City, the French founded an establishment there, which is occupied at present by the Abbé Couëdic, Dr. Quentin, the carpenter, the blacksmith and one of the two mechanics.

The inhabitants of the banza, mild and intelligent, have lent that personnel the collaboration of their arms. In less than two months, a new zeriba has been built outside the walls of the city. That fifth station is called René-Caillié, after the young voyager who went on foot from Senegal to Timbuktu and came back from Timbuktu to Tangier, in an era when no one had yet thought of exploring the African continent.[46]

The zeriba René-Caillié ought, by virtue of its situation, become a city of the first rank, perhaps the capital of Central Africa. It is the crossroads of the communicating route that extends from Saint Paul to Zanzibar and those that will not be long in linking the valley of the Zambezi to that of the Nile.

Commandant Beautemps-Fresnel left the Enchanted City on 1 May 1877, the fourth anniversary of Livingstone's death. Having descended the Tanganyika from north to south, he headed westwards along the line that was now marked out by the stations of Debaize, Compiégne, Le Saint and Maizan. When he returned,

---

[46] René Caillié (1799-1838) was the first European to reach Timbuktu and get back alive, in 1825. He went back in order to win a 10,000-franc prize offered by the Societé de Géographie, and again returned—only to die of tuberculosis almost as soon as he had settled down in France.

those already-flourishing stations envisaged the future in the most cheerful colors. The idea conceived by the late Admiral   seems sure to be realized in the near future.

Monsieur Fresnel reached Saint Paul de Loanda on 8 August 1877, the same day when Stanley arrived in Mboma, not far from the mouth of the Congo. The French expedition had therefore lasted no less than two years, two months and ten days.

Now the reader will doubtless be wondering what became of the characters who have had some role to play in the drama for whose action the Enchanted City served as a theater.

All the secondary agents of the expedition—the Pagazis, Kirangosis, Kabindards, Biribis and Hindu servants have been duly repatriated and generously recompensed for their long devotion. Chocolat is in Saint Paul, where he lives on his income, which consists of an honest regular ration of victuals. Every day he draws the amount due of that pension for life. He is the happiest of mulattos, and every day he offers San José de Cacuaco the expression of his actions and graces.

Mimoun is in Algeria. He lives in Medeah, where he fulfills the functions of a muezzin at the mosque of the Maliki rite. The good Muslim is content with his fate. One can hear him at daybreak calling the faithful to the fedjeur prayer, crying out to them in a nasal voice: "Allahu Akbar! Allahu Akbar!"

Thanks to his energy and the vigor of his constitution, Captain Harry Fox did not die of his wounds. After a long convalescence, the valiant officer of the Indian Army is in a satisfactory state of health. Having, of course, won his bet, Mr. Fox has become a millionaire. The geographical societies of London and Bombay have awarded him their great Gold Medal.

Commandant Fresnel and the engineer Duvivier are presently in Paris, where they are correcting the proofs of their travel journal.

Isidore is also in Paris, as anyone can see, for he is occupying the position of laboratory chef at the Hôtel Continental. A melancholy smile strays over his lips when he proceeds, in the morning, with the preparation of a cutlet à la Soubise, a preparation in which he succeeds marvelously. He then compares himself to the said Soubise, that great general of the Middle Ages, who had no more luck than he did, and who would have won the Battle of Rossbach…but for the fact that he lost it.

SF & FANTASY

Adolphe Alhaiza. *Cybele*

Alphonse Allais. *The Adventures of Captain Cap*

Henri Allorge. *The Great Cataclysm*

Guy d'Armen. *Doc Ardan: The City of Gold and Lepers*

G.-J. Arnaud. *The Ice Company*

Charles Asselineau. *The Double Life*

Henri Austruy. *The Eupantophone; The Olotelepan; The Petitpaon Era*

Barillet-Lagartousse. *The Final War*

Cyprien Bérard. *The Vampire Lord Ruthwen*

S. Henry Berthoud. *Martyrs of Science*

Aloysius Bertrand. *Gaspard de la Nuit*

Richard Bessière. *The Gardens of the Apocalypse; The Masters of Silence*

Albert Bleunard. *Ever Smaller*

Félix Bodin. *The Novel of the Future*

Louis Boussenard. *Monsieur Synthesis*

Alphonse Brown. *City of Glass; The Conquest of the Air*

Emile Calvet. *In a Thousand Years*

André Caroff. *The Terror of Madame Atomos; Miss Atomos; The Return of Madame Atomos; The Mistake of Madame Atomos; The Monsters of Madame Atomos; The Revenge of Madame Atomos; The Resurrection of Madame Atomos; The Mark of Madame Atomos; The Spheres of Madame Atomos; The Wrath of Madame Atomos* (w/M. & Sylvie Stéphan)

Félicien Champsaur. *The Human Arrow; Ouha, King of the Apes; Pharaoh's Wife*

Didier de Chousy. *Ignis*

Jules Clarétie. *Obsession*

Michel Corday. *The Eternal Flame*

André Couvreur. *The Necessary Evil*; *Caresco, Superman; The Exploits of Professor Tornada* (3 vols.)

Captain Danrit. *Undersea Odyssey*

C. I. Defontenay. *Star (Psi Cassiopeia)*

Charles Derennes. *The People of the Pole*

Georges Dodds (anthologist). *The Missing Link*

Charles Dodeman. *The Silent Bomb*

Harry Dickson. *The Heir of Dracula; Harry Dickson vs. The Spider*

Gustave Le Rouge. *The Mysterious Doctor Cornelius* (3 vols.); *The Vampires of Mars; The Dominion of the World* (w/Gustave Guitton) (4 vols.)

Jules Lermina. *Mysteryville; Panic in Paris; To-Ho and the Gold Destroyers; The Secret of Zippeliu; The Battle of Strasbourg*

André Lichtenberger. *The Centaurs; The Children of the Crab*

Jean-Marc & Randy Lofficier. *Edgar Allan Poe on Mars; The Katrina Protocol; Pacifica; Robonocchio; Return of the Nyctalope;* (anthologists) *Tales of the Shadowmen 1-10*

Xavier Mauméjean. *The League of Heroes*

Joseph Méry. *The Tower of Destiny*

Hippolyte Mettais. *The Year 5865; Paris Before the Deluge*

Louise Michel. *The Human Microbes; The New World*

Tony Moilin. *Paris in the Year 2000*

José Moselli. *Illa's End*

John-Antoine Nau. *Enemy Force*

Marie Nizet. *Captain Vampire*

C. Nodier, A. Beraud & Toussaint-Merle. *Frankenstein*

Henri de Parville. *An Inhabitant of the Planet Mars*

Gaston de Pawlowski. *Journey to the Land of the 4th Dimension*

Georges Pellerin. *The World in 2000 Years*

Ernest Pérochon. *The Frenetic People*

Pierre Pelot. *The Child Who Walked on the Sky*

J. Polidori, C. Nodier, E. Scribe. *Lord Ruthven the Vampire*

P.-A. Ponson du Terrail. *The Vampire and the Devil's Son; The Immortal Woman*

Edgar Quinet. *Ahasuerus; The Enchanter Merlin*

Henri de Régnier. *A Surfeit of Mirrors*

Maurice Renard. *The Blue Peril; Doctor Lerne; The Doctored Man; A Man Among the Microbes; The Master of Light*

Jean Richepin. *The Wing; The Crazy Corner*

Albert Robida. *The Adventures of Saturnin Farandoul; The Clock of the Centuries; Chalet in the Sky; The Electric Life*

J.-H. Rosny Aîné. *Helgvor of the Blue River; The Givreuse Enigma; The Mysterious Force; The Navigators of Space; Vamireh; The World of the Variants; The Young Vampire*

Marcel Rouff. *Journey to the Inverted World*

Han Ryner. *The Superhumans; The Human Ant*

Pierre de Selenes: *An Unknown World*

Angelo de Sorr. *The Vampires of London*

Brian Stableford. *The New Faust at the Tragicomique;The Empire of the Necromancers (The Shadow of Frankenstein; Frankenstein and the Vampire Countess; Frankenstein in London); Sherlock Holmes & The Vampires of Eternity; The Stones of Camelot; The Wayward Muse.* (anthologist) *News from the Moon; The Germans on Venus; The Supreme Progress; The World Above the World; Nemoville; Investigations of the Future; The Conqueror of Death; The Revolt of the Machines*

Jacques Spitz. *The Eye of Purgatory*

Kurt Steiner. *Ortog*

Eugène Thébault. *Radio-Terror*

C.-F. Tiphaigne de La Roche. *Amilec*

Louis Ulbach. *Prince Bonifacio*

Théo Varlet. *The Golden Rock. The Xenobiotic Invasion; The Castaways of Eros; Timeslip Troopers* (w/André Blandin); *The Martian Epic* (w/Octave Joncquel)

Paul Vibert. *The Mysterious Fluid*

Villiers de l'Isle-Adam. *The Scaffold; The Vampire Soul*

Philippe Ward. *Artahe ; The Song of Montségur* (w/Sylvie Miller) *Manhattan Ghost* (w/Mickael Laguerre)

MYSTERIES & THRILLERS

M. Allain & P. Souvestre. *The Daughter of Fantômas*

A. Anicet-Bourgeois, Lucien Dabril. *Rocambole*

A. Bernède. *Belphegor*; *Judex* (w/Louis Feuillade); *The Return of Judex* (w/Louis Feuillade); *The Shadow of Judex*

A. Bisson & G. Livet. *Nick Carter vs. Fantômas*

V. Darlay & H. de Gorsse. *Arsène Lupin vs. Sherlock Holmes: The Stage Play*

Séamas Duffy. *Sherlock Holmes in Paris*

Paul Féval. *Gentlemen of the Night; John Devil; The Black Coats ('Salem Street; The Invisible Weapon; The Parisian Jungle; The Companions of the Treasure; Heart of Steel; The Cadet Gang; The Sword-Swallower)*

Emile Gaboriau. *Monsieur Lecoq*

Goron & Emile Gautier. *Spawn of the Penitentiary*

Rick Lai. *Shadows of the Opera: Retribution in Blood; Sisters of the Shadows: The Curse of Cagliostro*

Steve Leadley. *Sherlock Holmes: The Circle of Blood*

Maurice Leblanc. *Arsène Lupin vs. Countess Cagliostro; Arsène Lupin vs. Sherlock Holmes (The Blonde Phantom; The Hollow Needle); The Many Faces of Arsène Lupin*

Gaston Leroux. *Chéri-Bibi; The Phantom of the Opera; Rouletabille & the Mystery of the Yellow Room; Rouletabille at Krupp's*

Richard Marsh. *The Complete Adventures of Judith Lee*

William Patrick Maynard. *The Terror of Fu Manchu; The Destiny of Fu Manchu*

Frank J. Morlock. *Sherlock Holmes: The Grand Horizontals; Sherlock Holmes vs Jack the Ripper*

Jean Petithuguenin. *The Adventures of Ethel King*

Antonin Reschal. *The Adventures of Miss Boston*

P. de Wattyne & Y. Walter. *Sherlock Holmes vs. Fantômas*

David White. *Fantômas in America*

Pierre Yrondy. *The Adventures of Thérèse Arnaud*

SCREENPLAYS

Mike Baron. *The Iron Triangle*

Emma Bull & Will Shetterly. *Nightspeeder; War for the Oaks*

Gerry Conway & Roy Thomas. *Doc Dynamo*

Steve Englehart. *Majorca*

James Hudnall. *The Devastator*

Jean-Marc & Randy Lofficier. *Royal Flush*

J.-M. & R. Lofficier & Marc Agapit. *Despair*

J.-M. & R. Lofficier & Joël Houssin. *City*

Andrew Paquette. *Peripheral Vision*

Robert L. Robinson, Jr. *Judex*

R. Thomas, J. Hendler & L. Sprague de Camp. *Rivers of Time*

NON-FICTION

Stephen R. Bissette. *Blur 1-5. Green Mountain Cinema 1; Teen Angels*

Win Scott Eckert. *Crossovers* (2 vols.)

Jean-Marc & Randy Lofficier. *Shadowmen* (2 vols.)

Randy Lofficier. *Over Here*